Francisco

FRANCISCO

Alison Mills Newman

Foreword by Saidiya Hartman

A NEW DIRECTIONS PAPERBOOK

First published by New Directions as NDP1554 in 2023
Manufactured in the United States of America

Library of Congress Cataloging-in-Publication Data
Names: Mills Newman, Alison, author.
Title: Francisco / Alison Mills Newman.
Description: New York, NY : New Directions Publishing Corporation, 2023.
Identifiers: LCCN 2022050524 | ISBN 9780811232395 (paperback) |
ISBN 9780811232401 (ebook)
Subjects: LCGFT: Novels.
Classification: LCC PS3563.I4235 F73 2023 |
DDC 813/.54—dc23/eng/20221026
LC record available at https://lccn.loc.gov/2022050524

2 4 6 8 10 9 7 5 3 1

New Directions Books are published for James Laughlin
by New Directions Publishing Corporation
80 Eighth Avenue. New York 10011

*This book is dedicated
to Nikki, Ted Jr., Morgan,
Mom, Dad, and May Ninth*

Contents

Foreword

This sensual and languorous autobiographical novel by Alison Mills Newman is a portrait of the artist as a young black woman trying to find a way back to herself: she is searching for an opening through which her capacities might be unloosened and where her talents will be actualized in accordance with her own designs. When we encounter the unnamed narrator, she has turned her back on worldly metrics of success. She has fled Hollywood with its saccharine integrationist television sitcoms and promises of ready stardom in black exploitation cinema. As she soon realizes, the belated invitation to the mainstream—even if as a noble token or as the only black friend or as a special guest appearance—demands assimilation as the price of the ticket. Her wanderings are devoted to unbecoming a successful Negro; her voyage directs her away from what she has been trained to want and toward other young artists in the Black Arts Movement, who want to be revolutionaries and not "Negro artists," who want to destroy the racial mountain rather than ascend it.

On an errant path toward the artist she might be, she is disinclined to strive because "trying is overrated." The novel might well be subtitled "In Praise of Idleness," conjuring the spirit of tool-breakers, recalcitrant domestics, shirkers, and strikers. The narrative drifts from moment to moment. Idleness, a refusal of the conditions of work, a refusal to be purposeful or dutiful, to strive or protest, feels liberating, especially after several years of working so very hard. "i be wanderin off sometimes—and when i come back i cannot tell you where i have been, cause i do not even know i was gone." The full elaboration of experience rather than a pedagogical impulse to explain the black world or describe it for outsiders enhances the textual pleasure of *Francisco*. Love, communion, intellectual debate, and aesthetic drive are the currents that shape its recursive movement. The drift and propulsion of the story feels like a '70s score, something Curtis Mayfield might have composed.

In this fugue state, she meets Francisco. The novel reads like a series of journal entries about the narrator's infatuation and love affair with Francisco. While Francisco "lives and breathes his work," the protagonist tries to find hers. Others call her lazy and unmotivated, accuse her of wasting her time; her father implores her to go to college and do something with her life. She appoints herself as muse. Yet, if there is breathing room in this love story of the Black Arts Movement, it emerges out of the category confusion about who exactly is the muse. She waxes lyrically about his beauty, his platform shoes, the trousers they share. He inspires her, less to make her own work, than to believe in his genius. Francisco is the kind of beautiful figure we find exalted on the canvas of a Barkley Hendricks painting.

It is here that the gender trouble of the novel arises in the unarticulated crisis of how she and Francisco might find a way to be together and love each other, outside of and liberated from the strictures of the imposed script of heterosexual romance, even in its bohemian variant. The ballad of Francisco and a young woman navigating aimlessness and actualization unfold with the elusive uncertainty of a latent text not yet able to articulate directly its questions about black women's lives and radical aesthetics and what it would mean for her to claim or to nurture her capacities, except in the form of observations and journal entries, except as admonitions from others about her purposeless and otiose existence, except as a chronicle of romance, or black love as an allegory of *what might be* (in the parlance of the day, *revolution*). She expresses doubt when reading an *Essence* magazine article about the great woman who stands behind the great man: "i don't know i think it's not so much behind every great man is a great woman, as much as a great man is a great man and a girl is a girl."

If the narrator is a muse of sorts, she is a complex one. She wants to do more than stand behind her man, even as she accepts that she takes second place after his commitment to his art. She knows the devotion and concentration required to make art. There are rare glimpses of her in this state of dedicated creation regarding her music. But mostly she pines for her lover, who doesn't make love when he works, though "maybe after the film is out and everythin we'll go away and make love all the time." Luckily, she is the kind easily distracted: a woman who puts eggs in the freezer, accidentally sets the trash can on fire, paints the refrigerator red, and lounges in bed reading James Weldon Johnson's *Black Manhattan*.

Francisco is an atlas of black culture in the 1970s and traces an itinerary from Harlem to Newark, from the Bay Area to Los Angeles, with Frank Silvera, Amiri Baraka, Angela Davis, Muhammed Ali, Pharoah Sanders, and Melvin Van Peebles as the cardinal points of the cultural map. David Henderson, Joe Overstreet, and Ishmael Reed appear as characters under pseudonyms. The novel is as much a chronicle of black artists as it is a love story. Sexual exploration and free love define the environment of the novel, yet the narrator's free-floating desire still seeks culmination in marriage. Her bohemianism has as its telos: husband and children and keeping house.

The vernacular language, the airy colloquial passages, and the fragmented structure defy any straight line of plot, derail *the girl meets great man and great man falls for girl* story, with numerous detours and pleasurable diversions. The text is episodic. Its meter languid and improvised. She and Francisco form one of those too beautiful couples like the dyads moving down the Soul Train Line. They float on top of the rhythm rather than dance, they ride it like the waves, like the ocean of James Brown's sound. The sheen of sweat on her skin makes her high brown even more beautiful and it is hard to know who to look at. Her or him? Who is prettier? He wears high-waisted velvet pants and silver platform shoes and turns more heads than she does in her slinky dress. He is sweet, yet unburdened, not at all haunted by the fear or guilty shame of what Baraka derided and embraced as "Negro faggotry." What is the playa if not a sweetback?

The story is dispersed across parties, film screenings, concerts, small gatherings, hanging with friends, and lots of lovemaking on sofas and in borrowed bedrooms. It is funny and irreverent: "we talked about revolutionists. i hate revolutionists … they all turn out to be movie stars in this country anyway"; "i couldn't think of no famous black man i wanted to fuck. once i wanted to fuck huey newton when i was sixteen, but not no more."

The wayward protagonist has found a muse in Francisco, or she might have if she allowed his genius to inspire her, or if she made him her second, or if she thought of him as a pleasurable indulgence, an extravagance, and not as essential for life. This brilliant beautiful young man is at the center of her meditations and reflections about power and blackness, art and revolution, love and liberation. Given the limits of the time and the world, and the femme self-effacement that is the bedrock of romance and the marriage plot, she casts herself as muse. For Francisco, the terms are otherwise. Women are a luxury, he tells her, and perhaps even an impediment to an aspiring young artist. When he is working on his film, he withholds, he sends her back home, he refuses to make love with her, underscoring the boundary between the first love—his film, his art— and his love for her. How she might be an artist *and* be with Francisco is the latent question of the novel, yet one too difficult to answer in the singular. It will require a collective response from a generation of black radical women and artists, from Toni Cade Bambara to Ntozake Shange.

Francisco anticipates Shange's *For Colored Girls Who Have Considered Suicide/When the Rainbow Is Enuf* and runs on a parallel track to Toni Morrison's *Sula* and Bambara's *Black Woman* anthology. While Sula's tragedy is that she is an artist without an art form and one who can only sublimate her yearning and want into an ardent desire for an ordinary man, Ajax, made mythic in her eyes, *Francisco* is neither a tragedy nor the blues (an *autobiographical chronicle of catastrophe expressed lyrically*), but rather a funky jam committed to pleasure and possibility. The searching young protagonist is certainly endowed with a sense of her artistry. Rather than work for the Man, she prefers to drift, not get stuck in place, to wake up at noon and make love on her friend's sofa, to raid her savings. (To fend off the extraction of her talents or the danger of being a "sold out afro" stoking the fantasies of white psychic life or feeding the insatiable racist appetites of Hollywood's libidinal machine, she devotes herself to Francisco.) The beauty of *Francisco* resides in this refusal to be dutiful to what she doesn't want: she rejects the imposed script. The risk is that aimlessness or insufficient devotion to her gifts all too easily yields to a love story about Francisco, where ardor and eros provide the cover for her self-abandonment, but since the novel is neither tragedy nor blues, the heroine escapes catastrophe as she journeys toward a melancholy self-embrace.

The unnamed narrator is a drifting young black woman who has walked away from success as a rising film and television star to find a means of expression or an opportunity for self-forgetting so that she might exceed the limited horizon of the world's expectation. To forget or exceed herself takes the form of erotic dissolution and spiritual oblation. This voluptuary tale has a theological undercurrent. The author's renouncement of the erotic adventure of *Francisco* in the afterword and testimony about finding God makes this clear. This, too, is in the tradition—Donna Summer renounced that *fall and free* way of love when she found Christ, as did Al Green. Is every god and goddess of love required to forsake their carnality to enter the kingdom, or to disown the Dionysian for the churchly? Are all the naughty girls and dissolute boys destined to become ascetics and monks? Must passion this intense yield to the divine, lend its force to the sacred? The spectral and the barely discernible devotions become manifest as Holy Ghost, though also borne in Malcolm X's stance and the Godfather of Soul's conk. Can I get a witness?

Certainly, the search for ecstasy assumes a secular form; it is very much in the flesh and *pussy* the valorized term of self-regard, and the slogan of a nascent black bohemian feminism, with Ntozake Shange wanting hers to get some sunlight, or bell hooks's fiery self-possession and declaration of struggle—whose is it, anyway?—or Audre Lorde coaxing it to delight with bananas, or Jamaica Kincaid's anti-heroine luxuriating in acts of autoeroticism and the smell of it in a world incapable of beholding black women, or the extended reprise of Ma Rainey and Bessie Smith bragging about the cosmic force of jelly rolls, or Jessie Fauset's plum bun proving that even bourgeois women can rock that thing, or Megan Thee Stallion and Cardi B authoring its anthem. Not unlike visionaries and mystics, martyrs and saints, the narrator's path to liberation is through self-erasure or subsumption in sublime experience. If this sounds like a marriage of the sensual and the spiritual, reader you are on the right track. If sex and self-immolation are tethered, it is because *Francisco* is a kindred spirit of Derek Jarman's *Sebastiane* or Carolee Schneeman's *Fuses* or Pasolini's *Teorema*. In plainer terms, what the young artist reaches for is transport; art and bodily experience provide the vehicle.

Devout self-abnegation recalls female mystics and martyrs for whom the willingness to sacrifice or forfeit the "I" is the pathway to greater knowledge and the divine. *Francisco* is heterodox in its beliefs and tentative in its commitments, so its portrait of a young artist in search of her path yields to female self-effacement and the muse's desire to live through the genius of her man. It is important to note that Francisco does not demand this of her, rather it is what she offers. He, in turn, helps her to love herself, to love her smell, to love the eruptions of the funk that the bourgeois black daughter had been disciplined to repel, if not loathe. The tension of the novel is between the femme's self-abasing love for the brilliant masculine creator and the artist in search of her own form. It is a story of sexual transgression, not because it is scandalous, but because it defies the tenets of respectability which have provided the pillars of black striving. The narrator, literally and figuratively, resides in her father's house. He is an accomplished scientist who takes for granted his daughter's soon-to-be achievements in the world, and that her strict upbringing has decided her course. The rules and prohibitions of the father's house are explicit, and no less ardent is the daughter's desire to flounce those rules, to indulge in acts of intimate trespass; want and reckless desire lead to her lover's bed, yet for the sake of appearance and the need of propriety she returns to her own room by dawn.

In Francisco, she finds a partner also in the search for liberation; like her, he finds beauty in the black ordinary and reveres everyday folks and their ways of surviving and enduring the world—sprawling conversations about revolution on a bus ride through the city, sisters sketching designs for a new planet as they fry chicken and do hair, or black commoners experimenting with ways not to be a Negro in the white man's world. The extraordinary beauty of black folks everywhere apparent is inextricable from the *what* and *how* of liberation. Their aesthetic experiment is an experiment in living—how is it that one might be black and free? She and Francisco learn how *not* to strive, how not to step onto the path awaiting the black elite, and instead to yearn for something better and more substantial than money or success or fame.

The freedom to eschew protest or uplift in the search for a zone in which one might enjoy the pleasures of everyday life, from the sonic rootwork of James Brown to an afternoon tryst, where sexual pleasure is inseparable from the veneration of blackness and the transport and the potentiality of sweaty bodies in a circle. James Brown's *Cold Sweat* is the ur-text of this possibility: *everything was in union with us.*

The pace of the narrative, its black groove, the dissident resonance of free jazz, the pulse and vibration of a liberation now suite, its all-encompassing eros is a testament of black potentiality in flux—the shift from revolutionary icons and political parties with armed wings—toward an open-ended and expectant sense that anything might be possible despite the disappointment that the revolution has not yet come to pass. The anticipation and the hope are ubiquitous and set the tone of ordinary life. Despite the celebrity revolutionaries, no one person or party exercises a sovereign claim or copyright to the black movement against the given, unfolding in the streets, in black arts, in carnal acts.

The narrator finds a place alongside black male genius, by loving and nurturing it. Her aimlessness enables her to be what she might need to be and on the ready. Francisco doesn't make her his muse; fascinated by his genius, she relinquishes herself to him. Fleeing everything she was, she meets Francisco in the throes of this self-abandonment. She has turned her back on everything that she is supposed to want: money, celebrity, fame. She has turned her back on being a representative Negro, on being a daughter of Europe, on loving whiteness, and by so doing, she both finds a friend in her bed and learns to love herself dearly, even as the world fails to love her. Her arms provide a refuge, often the only one possible. So, this no-longer muse learns to keep company with herself. It is the gift yielded by the errant path.

SAIDIYA HARTMAN

Francisco

Part I

I Wanted to Make It When I Realized I Couldn't Fly

my jazzman don't know how to sing.
he don't know nothin bout no woodwinds
drums, no brass, no strings.
but he's so fine
his music's in his eyes
and he plays what he sees
with a funky saxophone sheen
on the silver screen.

i got up at eleven this mornin after layin round, rollin round in the bed, huggin round in the bed with this friend of mine. i say friend cause i ain't heard him qualify the relationship yet.

i've heard girlfriend which does not exactly appeal to me. besides in all nonbullshit, friend is the truest and best word.

so me and my friend hugged all mornin long, till i gave him one good feel of my roundness and softness just to make sure he was hard and on and got up to clean the kitchen and it was a mess cause after a night ride alone to sausalito and north beach by my own self cause i was pissed cause he gave me some shiny brown pants of his and then took them back three

hours later cause he saw how much i like them and decided
there must be somethin to them after all, and tried them on
his own self to discover he liked them too, yeah—well i came
back at twelve thirty and there he lay on the couch watchin
dick cavett run off at the mouth and i said you want somethin
to eat?
you can always get a nigga through food.

so i layed down this food stamp list of things we had—the list
bein almost listless. there was some watermelon some eggs,
some chicken left ova, some liva and some toast. he settled on
toast. i came in the kitchen with my twenty-one-year-old self
made some cinnamon toast and brought it out to him with a
glass of milk. he liked it. i like to see him eat the stuff i fix with
such enjoyment and when he asks for more, it kills me so i
came back in the kitchen and made some more—the second
batch wasn't as good as the first, but in the meantime i messed
up the kitchen cause i am not neat at this kind of stuff.

now after fixin this man some breakfast who refuses to empty
the trash, there are three bags overflowin full sittin by the icebox lopsided, and one big huge can of trash whose top will
not close—and i guess he expects me to do it—while he sits
on that high stool in his bedroom editing his film. he's crazy.

he doesn't make love when he works, and since i've known
him he's been workin on this film of his. i mean, we did, and
all the first three or four nights of our relationship dangerously
cause i don't take no birth control pills (i can't stand them
things) and after he went away to n.y. the whole week passed
and i wondered if i was, but then upon his return my period

was ova, cause mine only last a day or two if that, sometimes an hour—

and we didn't have no baby that time.

but then as our relationship grew so did our practicality and we refrained but some of this refrainin is too much for me. i mean, i get highly frustrated flyin back and forth from l.a. to s.f. and not gettin none from this fine black specimen ceptin now and then.

but he works hard. i can feel it: when he gets into bed at night he's dead almost before he closes his eyes and manages a few goodnight words. he pulls me to him and holds me softly, and i think we wake up thataway, then the fight begins. we talk about carcinogen in foods causing cancer, and film. i made a bet with him that his film would win some kind of an award. cannes film festival, new york critics. i don't care about hollywood awards. they can have them.

the film is called *ain't nobody slick,* but i think francisco thinks he is. it includes in its story angela davis who francisco interviewed while in jail.

francisco got this cameraman who lives in sausalito to shoot his movie, michel cerf. a short, thin, stylish tennis shoed, tanned, army jacketed, scarf around neck frenchman who doesn't like american women, generally. he says he finds american women to be boring and stupid—without class or style—he says the french woman is required to be charming, somethin that the american woman lacks. he likes me though, and later a friend

of mine named chris joy—a vivacious, always-on-stage actress, five-foot-two blonde animal girl who has a haircut like
jane fonda, or shall i say jane fonda got a haircut like her. chris
looks like jane fonda in a ways a little—and francisco flew
her up (from l.a. where she lives) to be in the movie cause he
wanted a girl to be in this rich nouveau chic decadent revolutionary white black scene, and he wanted a girl to suggest
jane fonda.

i don't think very much of jane fonda. i mean in a time when
malcolm x and martin luther king came and lived and made
such a true commitment—they didn't have no rich white
nothin to return to—nothin to lose and everything to gain by
freakin off at some neurotic need to find somethin supposedly
constructive to do; when men and women lived and died so
niggas could just wake up and remember who they are, what
they come from, what they allowin to be done to them, and
what they doin to themselves. i mean just so if you saw another
nigga comin in your midst you wouldn't have to go hide in the
bathroom, ashamed of your own content, or image.

yeah, i could go on but that would only be borin since most
people done forgot about everything that went down or up
anyway, or too scared to do what they really want to do, and
upon hittin forty go around saying if i had only had a chance.
besides everybody's been bought.

but it amazes me how some white girl can tell black men that
they are weak if they don't all carry guns. does she carry a gun?
if so, so what. with her popcorn hollywood silva screen men-
tality.

life ain't no hollywood production (no matter how much money they might spend to make me think it is).

to even go to the academy awards and receive a trophy from the very same people that helped dilute the images of black people — of people who contribute to the very same existence that she is so strongly tryin to change. (you can't be everything to everybody, you end up being nothin to everybody.)

so chris joy came to do the part. we found her a really great dress — a bright 1930 slit out in the back boss red dress to wear in the film. we found it in a little antique shop in north beach — just an hour or two before shooting time.

chris and i left the house early (francisco was filmin a blood and violence police versus panther raid in his bedroom) and i drove us down to north beach in francisco's ladybug blue volkswagen. we had salad and wine and talked about old times and new times comin at enrico's and somehow we escaped two black men (one was young, about twenty with wavy stockin cap slicked down do, baggy pants meetin some half tied tongue hangin out wornout tennis shoes, grinnin under his chest in a soiled white t-shirt, slightly high and ready. the otha man at least forty, stinky, crazy, alley-slime smellin piss drunk. red eyes streaked and stuck on a wine wrinkled puffed cheeked black face. he must have worked with his hands all his life cause they were somethin big and strong and viciously grinded in dirt. his toes were covered in raggedy tennis shoes, half tied too).

they followed us around in and out of shops, harassin me bout how i probably had a white man waitin for me at home, and then later askin me if they could buy me somethin pretty and take me home, after accusin me of being a dyke.

chris and i managed to get back to cole street after gettin lost several times due to wrong direction givers, after trying to lose those two black men who had the nerve to follow us in their 1950 scratched dulled green pickup junk truck.

francisco was gonna shoot the party scene ova at a million-aire's house in Berkeley. a rich white lady who married quen-tin, this black man.

quentin who is about fifty now or so, thin spry and cool in his tapered moustache walkin around in italian house slippas and a dashiki his wife made him, is finally supa pimp.

but anyway,
their house is great and so are they—though i heard two days later that quentin pulled a gun on sarah—sarah that's his wife, she's a kind, wrinkled face woman in her late sixties, also thin, dressed in pants, and stylish house slippers—her hair is sprinkled grey brown hangin loosely free down to her shoul-ders, her forehead covered with short bangs. sarah jumped everytime quentin called her in his demanding King of the Konk Tone. and sarah could always go skinnin and grinnin, drippin in joy happily, droppin whatever she happened to be doin callin ... yes baby. i hear you baby. i'm on my way baby.

and francisco got ba.
this big gleamin nigga who dances with this famous dance group in s.f. and has his own dance studio to come around and

be in the movie. ba got a ring in his ear, and is so gloriously, ravenously black with this thick deep gay roarin comin from the belly laughter celebrated in flamboyant theatrics flarin in everythin he does—i mean in the way he dresses, talks, walks, sneezes, shakes your hand, enters a room, leaves a party, picks up a glass, greets you, and bids you a goodbye. ba is one marvelous big eyed dude, with bright teeth.

so ba came around to be in the movie, and put a hot dog bun on his private parts with mustard and ketchup after sniffin cocaine a mountain high in the form of C and H sugar.

a whole bunch of get down cow down friends and strangers came too. all of whom were perfectly willin to be filmed and act a little extra out there for the party scene. jonathan came ova. he's a friend of mine i met in n.y. i understand why he didn't want to be in that particular scene. it did get intentionally raunchy.

i helped chris get dressed, and told her how she looked beautiful and stuff, and michel cerf tried to hit on her, as did some otha dudes and francisco was in his own world discussin with michel cerf how they were gonna shoot the party scene. francisco puts all his energy—everythin into his work. for the first time i realized how he lived and breathed his work. sometimes i watched him without his knowin.

there was plenty of wine to drink. and drink we did. and dance? lord—folks were dancin, fallin all ova the couch—the music was loud, jimi hendrix was there sometimes on record, quentin was havin a grand time dancin and eyein the young ladies passin by him in his castle. well alright, he would murmur to a pair of passin legs in high heels. well alright!

i went in this bedroom on the first floor, in sarah's house. all by myself watchin t.v., and then sarah's daughta, elaine aged twelve, with long blonde hair that she wore in two thick braids—big blue eyes, joined me. we watched t.v. together. we cracked up at some of the commercials. especially the ones advertisin tires that would last so many miles—when even she knew they had tires that would probably never wear out.

francisco came and found me. he wanted me to come out and join the party scene (he was very pleased with the dress i had convinced chris to buy, but he wondered why i hadn't bought myself a dress) ... so i did. i danced. i danced till my body was loose and i could feel these lights—these electrical currents comin out of me. see, i love to dance, i love to dance in the rain. somethin in my spirit just comes alive when i'm dancin.

exavier invited an asian girlfriend of his to come ova. she came ova and peeped through the window with this girlfriend of her, and they asked—what kind of a party is this? somethin out of la dolce vita? she and her friend didn't come in.

but she came ova the next day cause see francisco and exavier were invited to bed the night ova sarah's and quentin's after all the shootin was ova, cause we was too tired to drive back to s.f. so exavier called his friend up in the mornin and invited her ova. he had to do some heavy convincin that nothin would happen to her. marsha's her name. she is a tall girl, with one cracked tooth, thick shoulder length asian jet black hair, lots of make-up on, and talks like a blood. so we spent the mornin tellin her how the party was crazy and all just for a scene in this movie — she cracked up and so did we.

exavier just came ova tap dancin and singin, What it is!

exavier got a friend named john with him — a cocker spaniel eyed, thirtyish, emaciated, boneylegged dude, in a green army uniform. before john says anything in a conversation, he'll tilt his head and say,
pardon me, but dig this.

exavier is in the movie too. exavier is friend, actor, college student, husband, father, and mysterious character. he's francisco's friend. we hang out together ova here sometimes on cole street, where francisco lives and me now.

francisco got rid of boopsy his cousin, who's always high on somethin tip toein around with his light-skinned wavy haired wanting to serve biosexual self.

boopsy lives from place to place. he lived with francisco free for six months and francisco finally put him out cause he didn't neva get no job or nothin and contribute to his own existence.

boopsy dropped ova yesterday when francisco and exavier sat me down in the kitchen and started gettin on my case cause i had gone away and locked francisco out and he had to climb up the side of the house to pry open a window so he could get in and work on his film.

boopsy told us that he had gotten a job as a ginny pig. some doctors or somebody are gonna give him drugs, and experiment on him and stuff—he gets three hundred dollars and free room and board for thirty days. francisco said that was good, at least you're gonna get paid for what you do.

francisco is in his bedroom now. you should see him. he looks like a mad man. a mad scientist or somethin with all those little strange instruments in front of him. a little cardboard screen, he looks like a natural nut sittin all hunched up on a stool with the bedroom blinds closed, editin his film, choppin his film up, crackin up at the music, lovin the people in the scenes, talkin-cussin to himself. sometimes i go in there, and i don't go in there often cause he tells me to get out—or not to step on the film.

i went to the park and picked some flowers and exercised my body for a taste, and then drove home and started comparin my feet to francisco's. his is the color of my face and my feet are the color of his face—i'm a yellow nigga. a freckled face nigga. you know, you've seen our kind. he asked me if bloods use to eva make fun of my freckles and i said naw,

but white folks did—i used to go read for parts and stuff— they used to look at me wonderin like—niggas got freckles too? and once when i went to private school in n.y., the white folks made me out to be everythin else otha than black. some of them would ask me if i was greek, indian, anything—but black.

i don't know,
then there was a time in elementary school

now i remember
if you black and freckled and light with wavy hair you good
black—and if you othawise the direct opposite—bad. that
was only in limited circles howeva—sometimes dark black
kids hated light black kids, and vice versa, but not me.

i don't know
i just didn't think very much of my physicalness and nobody
else did either. i wasn't considered to be cute or nothin. i could
have been though if i hadn't of worn the same clothes everyday. i mean my parents were well off lived in a big house with
a swimmin pool, middle class blacks and could of bought me
clothes and did. i just didn't wear them. i used to wear this
woolen grey sweater and woolen grey skirt everyday. and besides i wasn't interested in no boys. i liked men.

my friends use to be surprised when for the first time they
would come ova my house. they thought i was poor. i looked
like i didn't belong to myself much less two good parents.

anyway
then i came in the kitchen and put these flowers in this vase
amongst all this shit on the kitchen table, and started thinkin
about how i first met francisco ova tad's house. tad's an artist,
a great painter. tad is one burly big beer stomached, honest
sloven beautiful greasy-silky haired nigga-NEGROW.

tad took me ova his house, from jonathan's cottage where i was
staying all by my own self, which was just what i needed. there
was a piano, candles, and i could play the piano late at night—
there were lots of books, books on everything african, pictures
of egyptian monuments, figures, and fleas. it was a little cabin

house stuck behind this main house where this bare foot college couple lived with their mud faced gigglin child. i got into straightening the cottage up, and decoratin it a little.

tad took me ova his house to eat dinna, and hang out—and meet his wife and family cause see i had neva met them before, though i had heard lots about them in n.y. when tad was there a couple of years ago for an art gallery showin of his works.

tad started gettin into a philosophical discussion about makin it, and how i couldn't change the world, and how it was nice to have all these idealistic ideas, but they would just be ideas (Sung to you by HARRY CROONER AND THE *Sooner or Laters*), and i'd come to know the stark ugly Truth of the world as is, and always will be PERIOD. and then

Knock Knock on the door
and tad said opening it,
Here comes one nigga who thinks he can change the world. he was tall and dark brown with a conquistador moustache with some blue corduroy pants on, some kind of yellow and red striped sweater—and those shoes. he had on some blue shoes that had this yellow tongue stickin out of a red mouth with thick wooden heels, and i loved those shoes. i had a light for francisco just behind those crazy shoes. he walked through that door with such vigor and perseverance and life, man.

but he didn't pay me no mind. i was all in black again, with my hair all out wavy bushed parted in the middle woolyfied lookin unheard of, and one of my eyes was bloodshot.

tad and francisco talked some business for a while after i was brushingly half introduced. this was after francisco had been in the house ten minutes already. i said hi. he said hi, and then went on talkin to tad.

well. i went in the kitchen to talk about dietin with tad's wife, jennifer—who is also a piscean like me. jennifer was so lovely, and warm just as i had heard she was from people who had known her (that i met) in n.y.

francisco was into his film talkin bout this and that—he wanted tad to make some posters or somethin, and then they finished talkin and settled down to eat some tuna fish sandwiches—i was still in the kitchen laughin with jennifer, and enjoyin their two beautiful big eyed sons both under twelve. they were runnin round being delightful smart bad children when francisco looked at me—and me him.

johnathan called and told me to wait for him outside cause he was comin to get me to take me out to dinna with his friends and felipe luciano who was on his way to china. we would have a farewell dinna.

but johnathan didn't feel like gettin out of the car to come in the house—so i said okay, and hung up the phone and kissed tad and jennifer goodbye and francisco—who ignored the kiss, and me when i happened to mention where i was stayin.

oh i was so embarrassed as i closed the door behind me, and waited out on the front porch only to return cause johnathan didn't come as usual. he didn't come till two hours later.

so i sat down in a chair, and francisco asked me to be in his next film cause in between all this action somehow it slipped out bout me bein an actress, in theatre and t.v., on all those tired t.v. shows, and specials with my guest starring role self, and about some movie i was gonna do, if it eva got done. francisco said actors needed a challenge, and that was for true. who doesn't? that's why i was excited about doin that film that james oliver is supposed to direct, cause i thought it would be good. but it sure was funny bein called an actor, cause it wasn't that i didn't like t.v., but i didn't like what i did on t.v. too tough. there were a few experiences i had, and very few they were—where i got the chance to create and do somthin—those shows were usually canceled.

on one t.v. show i worked on at age seventeen (one of the first t.v. series that a black woman starred in), i remember askin the producer if i could wear my own hair, cause he had me wearin a long fall that fell all down my back and hit midway in the center of my behind.

well, wasn't nobody white in america wearin their hair like that, much less black, and even if they were if he wanted long hair i had long hair at the time, and so i asked him one day on the set, if i could please stop wearin that wig, cause i was seventeen playin a seventeen-year-old girl, and what was wrong with my own hair? that man looked me straight in the eye and said my hair looked like rats had been suckin on it. i should of known i was working for a man who was makin a fortune off a people he thought so little of.

i didn't like films that had been made within the last onslurge of black slop. and i was glad i hadn't been in none of them, besides i didn't give a fuck—i'd rather starve than do something i didn't

believe in and i didn't start actin to make no million dollars. i
started when i was twelve after beggin and pleadin—and then
with the assistance of my mother—cause i was gonna die if i
didn't cause i love the theatre and film and t.v. and all of it—and
i wanted to do somethin beautiful, somethin that i could—

tad told me to shut up

but i went on talkin bout how i had done things in my considered to be successful times—times when i made a lot
of money, lived in a big great house in nichols canyon, and
walked recognized on the streets—but i wanted to protect my
gift, my talent given me, and how up to a time that meant the
inability to do things on a certain financial level

and how that day

when i was nineteen and my car wouldn't start and i called
the automobile club of america to come fix it, and they sent
this old black man in a rickety truck drivin up the windin hollywood hills bein passed by fast stormin m.g.'s and long slinky
ego rolls royce's till he got to my house hidden behind some
thick shrubbery that i shared with nancy, my best friend at the
time—aspiring actress.

it was hot that day. i fixed some lemonade at the suggestion
of bowlegged, stringy-haired, good soul white girl nancy—i
sat out in the front yard driveway and talked to that old black
man while he repaired my car. that old man was music. he had
a cap on his head, polka dotted in filth and grease. he'd tap his
cap every now and then in a rhythmical beat. he had neva seen
me on t.v., which was a nice feelin—he was so beautiful. a rich

skinned blues black man, you could tell he worked out doors a lot in the sun, cause his face was so shiny leathered, his hands showed he must have worked hard all his life. the smile was like the root of a tree, so deep, so alive, so nurtured in light. i could see him sitting jolly at a bar, his cap before him on the table. i could see him sittin in a church funky baptist pew, rocking to some gospel on fire humble soul singers. i wanted to ask him desperately what gave him so much peace, what was that joy? but a suffocating shyness came out of nowhere and choked me, held me back. he got in his truck and drove down the driveway past the bushes and trees. i fought the inexplicable hindrance, broke free and ran down the hill in an expectant, hopeful rush to ask him the question on my heart but in a poof he and his truck were gone.

i stood paralyzed

confused

wondering how he could have disappeared so suddenly as the earth shook and rattled beneath me, and i heard a commanding soft voice from within say, the point is, alison, there goes a real star.

how could that old man be a star? nobody knows his name. he's not famous, rich, he's no celebrity on the cover of magazines.

i'm not a star?

shaking, i ran up the hill to the living room in my house and stared out over the hills looking through the sliding glass windows and saw marilyn monroe and dorothy dandridge

Dying.

i shook my head ... no ... no

No. SCREAMING NO!

i called my agent at caa and said i was leaving for new york.
are you in love? he asked
no, i weeped. if i stay in hollywood i'm gonna die, i said hysterically ... i'm gonna die.
he hung up the phone.

the next morning i was in n.y. i worked in n.y. with walter jones,
dick williams, and did a one-act play at imamu amiri baraka's
spirit house in new jersey, and worked at the house of kuumba
with the black magicians, celebrated my first kwanza, and did
plays by unknown playwrights off broadway. i only made fifteen dollars a night, and sometimes nothin—a far cry from
a thousand a week. i lived like boopsy—from place to place.

francisco let it be known that he wanted my phone number in
l.a. cause he would be comin down there. he gave me his phone
number (before him and tad left to go out and get somethin to
drink somewheres. me—still waitin for johnathan) so i could
call him the next day cause he couldn't call me, cause there
wasn't no phone in johnathan's cottage.

so i left berkeley, and went home to l.a. it was my first time
in berkeley and i liked johnathan and tad's city. it had been
good to me. johnathan had been good to me, my beautiful
poet friend. i needed the rest.

so one evenin, maybe two or three weeks later, francisco calls
me. i didn't believe it. i mean i was surprised. and he sounded
so great ova the phone. he sounded like a kid. i couldn't see
him the first night he called, or the second night. we finally got
together one hot afternoon.

he came to my father's house. i was a nervous wreck before he got there tryin to figure out what to wear. mostly everything was dirty—but i changed several times in and out of one thing, into another. i kept on what i had on in the first place.

he liked my father's house. it reminded him of a spanish villa. he lived in italy once. been all ova europe. he was stayin with his uncle who was a lawyer, living out in hermosa beach, while he was in town takin care of business at c.f.i. he invited me ova his uncle's house for dinna. i said okay, and went upstairs to change again. doubled up between the blankets of my unmade bed. i found my lovely blue 1940 long dress that has four pearl buttons down the front. it is one of the best dresses i have. i mean i didn't have no holes in it yet. cause most of my clothes are old and fallin apart. rags. that's my style. francisco says i make rags look expensive and i'd probably make somethin expensive look like a rag.

francisco was wearin his long brown hairy legs, and brown hair tinted golden red in spots by the sun. black adonis in shorts—his feet in leather sandals, and anotha multicolored t-shirt on.

i came downstairs and fumbled through some mail sittin on the bar—francisco leaned ova gentle and kissed me on my cheek. i was gone. i was shocked that he was in my house, that he kept callin me even though i had said no twice. i was surprised that he even remembered me, or bothered to call me. i mean i was out. where did he come from all of a sudden?

so we left my dad's house, after i introduced him to my dad

who reacted rather coldly. another nigga, oh lord. i guess my
father must have been thinkin.

but our mood was not disturbed. we drove along the highway
to the beach engaged in our high, talkin a mile a minute.

what really happened in hollywood?
why did you leave and go to n.y. when you had it made?
i shrugged my shoulders and gazed out the car window listening to the sound of the thrashing healing ocean waves.
i sang ever so softly.
i saw the ocean shining, i walked along its crystal light of good-
ness smiling.

i didn't want to rememba my encounters with old fat gray-
haired baldheaded producers
at major motion studios
telling me of their pleasure of choosing me to star in their great
script written with me in mind comparing me to dorothy dandridge and marilyn monroe
disappearing into their luxurious office bathroom only to return naked lying on the floor and playing with themselves,
inviting me to join them, making it unmistakably clear the
repulsive act was required to secure the advancement of my
already promising career.
i'm an actress, not a prostitute, i youthfully protested.
scruples? you won't go far the old/young slimy producers/
directors in mocking montages laughed. i didn't want to rememba telling my mother who didn't believe me, confiding
in older, actress friends who encouraged me to do it, play the
game. i wasn't strong enough to rememba my deep buried

graveyard heartbroken confusion wondering if i was the crazy one? suicidal meditations stalking me in the valley of decision. it was too achingly painful to summon up the memory of being blackballed by hollywood babylon traumatized and alone in my election to not conform.

i love your voice, i love the way you sing . . . francisco contemplated out loud in an amorous tone of comforting support, intuitively understanding. we laughed together in a chill vibe the question foreva slain.

i almost got married. just about a month ago. i don't see why girls can't be friends with men, the way the girls are with girls, you know? sometimes i would walk down the street with this friend of mine in n.y.—this girl, my arm through hers, and people would think i was a lesbian. it's a shame how people think thataway about stuff. i mean i use to hold my sista's hand when we walked down the street togetha. i didn't get married, cause this guy kept relatin to me out of the past. i had known him two years before, and just returned. i kept tellin me, that ain't me no more. i mean that's a part of me, but there's other parts added on to me now. he didn't love the me. i like the idea of marriage. of bein with one person and growin together. why did you go to berkeley? to get away.

francisco said in his coolness, he might marry me. my eyes bugged like nigga's eyes in the movies did in the old days when a nigga be talkin to the white man or white lady of the house.

his uncle lived in a nice house, with his new orleans lookin type wife, and his nine-year-old light brown blonde haired daughter.

we ate crabs that didn't come out too good, and drank some dubonnet wine, listenin to mose allison and ray charles. later his uncle, francisco, and i went to the light house, a jazz joint in hermosa beach (while his uncle's wife went to bed).

pharoah sanders was playin that night. all that good music flyin, people ease. ornette coleman—made me feel like i was in n.y., down near the lowa east side. made me think about goin to slugs one night, and listenin to ornette coleman blow on his saxophone. i rememba lookin at francisco and feelin like a twelve-year-old kid.

where'd you come from? i asked as i hugged francisco warmly.

he laughed.

the show ova, his uncle drove us home. uncle harold, anotha high-yeller, slightly mexican lookin nigga. seems like francisco's the darkest one in his family that i've seen so far. most of francisco's family is pink yella.

so there's harold drivin along in his candy brown mercedes and me thinkin this is the life.

we got to his home, harold goes to bed, francisco and i watch t.v. then francisco turns the t.v. off, undresses me, slowly unbuttoning the four buttons down the front of my dress. my shoes, my underwear, his own clothes. we made love on the couch. we made love on nothin but couches for such a long time. most of the time ova my daddy's house. we'd sleep together on the couch and then francisco would get up and leave before six a.m.—before my dad woke up to go to work. we never slept in a bed together till he brought me to his house in s.f.

francisco made a sly remark about my underwear havin a odor, in the mornin. i laughed—i'm gonna get you. i said. i hope you do, he said smilin as he watched my booty. he loves my booty. i'm gonna put my booty in his mind.

i played songs for him ova my father's house. i turned off all the lights downstairs, and lit candles. i put one candle on the piano, so i could see what i was playin, and one near francisco, as he lay on the couch in the den. i played. i was dressed all in white that night.

francisco showed me his film at a screenin room on the ucla campus. i thought his film was good. i was totally impressed but was honestly bored with angela. maybe it had a lot to do with her bein in jail and what that environment does to a person, maybe. but at the same time, i was amazed by her. francisco had her smilin sometimes—the cigarette stains on her teeth showed up. she looked hard sometimes, very hard— but her hands were soft, at otha times there was this vision of strength and beauty, and a great mental control.

i wondered about her when she talked about marxism in reference to a socialistic way of livin. a community way of co-operatin with each otha. i questioned her. i questioned her knowledge of herself, of her people. why should she have to refer to marxism to back up her statements, when she could refer to her own heritage, to africa, to a time a place a people that existed before marx was thought of—i mean i didn't see what he had to do in the matter. i mean she could refer to a whole culture, history, that was her own. francisco called her the daughter of europe, later he told me she was a girl scout.

someone who knew her before the famous days said she was a nice girl, unmaterialistic, use to wear the same coat everywhere she went, and drive around in an old beat up car. and would probably never have any money contrary to the hierarchy in the panther organization.

but whatever her statement, her stand, her strength if not questioned as to its background, is a stand, a strength and integrity i respect and admire her much for takin, and so i left it at that.

after the film i saw, i thought how she has a great opportunity to do somethin—but i never got the feelin of a high spiritual force—i mean malcolm x and martin luther king were circulating alive spirit men who captured the sense of worth, minds, spirits, souls, dreams, hearts, hopes of people magically.

francisco loves james brown.
it's true. francisco lives in san francisco. francisco trips out behind james brown the way i trip out behind wheat germ, and old upright pianos slightly out of key. francisco is the only nigga i know who defies bein typecast. i mean, he's a graduate of stanford (tho, the only reason he went to stanford after being president of berkeley high so nobody would fuck with him). which is understandable cause one night when i was in l.a. my dad called me into his bedroom and asked me who he was, and what did he do, and i went on with all that jazz about

him makin a film, being a director and all which did not all make my father too happy, and then i mentioned,

and he's a graduate of stanford

which made my father relax a little and settle back like the world was in order at last.

both my parents are college educated. i am not. i never went cept for a couple of weeks at l.a. city college. i had to drop out cause i got a part in a t.v. series, and didn't feel like doin both. sometimes i'd go visit big legged linda jones, a scholarly bright friend of mine from high school, when she was going to stanford university. i liked visitin school, but i can't imagine goin to one. they usually look like prisons to me, but then i haven't really seen a prison cept on t.v.

i've lectured at colleges about actin, and read poetry, and done plays at different colleges since age twelve. but i've never attended a college any length of time as an enrolled student.

but you know yesterday ova carla's house, this friend of mine also from high school days who knows how extremely round, silent, reserved, and unattractive i used to be—carla lives up in baldwin hills in her parents' house. well francisco came and got me—and he sat down to talk to carla cause carla is fine, and the mother acted like francisco wasn't even human cause he did look like some stray funky beautiful nigga with his hair all uncombed. and then carla and francisco started sharin their experiences about stanford, and carla asked francisco when did he graduate, and that lady perked up like an electrical fuck hit

her and got all excited and purrin openin up and talkin to francisco all warm and friendly, offerin him food, ginger ale, wine.

francisco is crazy about james brown. i mean he actually goes
out and buys his records. i mean even exavier thinks it's strange.
and couldn't too much be strange to exavier cause he is really
strange to me. i mean exavier wears these painters' hats on his
square head all the time, is gonna be a lawyer, i mean he goes
to college at s.f. state, and got some kind of degree in psychol-
ogy from some college somewheres, use to be a gangster in
n.y., use to be a heroin addict, is always spotlessly immaculate,
knows everybody that is suppose to have eva been anybody, or
still is or might be somebody someday and i don't know him
or where he lives, cause he don't work, but he's always busy
and got at least three credit cards, drives a brand new car. he
just disappears in and disappears out.

francisco just came in here. the floor is mopped so he has to
tiptoe him in his black multi-colored stripes of blue red and
yella t-shirt. francisco likes bright colors.

i could kick his ass. i asked him to take the trash out and i
ended up doin it. i don't want to say anythin. well maybe i
should. no i won't.

i started to read this story out of essence magazine. a story about
black women and how behind every successful man there is a
woman who could probably be successful herself. that's true i
guess. but then i don't know no man that got just one woman.
i mean most of these men must have passed through lots of
could-be successful women. so what does that mean?

well, i don't know how francisco would feel about all this. but i won't say nothin.

cause he works hard on his film, and the next film he wants to do, and i understand how that is cause when i work on music that's all i can think about is the song. and i just understand cause it takes a lot of concentration to get anything done. and maybe men don't get any fun out of life till after they've worked. then they go crazy. and maybe after the film is out and everythin we'll go away and make love all the time.

i don't know but i know the kitchen is clean now. the trash is out. he gave me those pair of shiny brown pants and i wore them downtown with him today. and i wish i could eat and neva gain a pound, and i wish people who made all these movies responded to quality more often. i mean, i wish some of this copy cat copy would disappear now and then. but folks don't seem to produce quality on purpose, they dilute it till it don't exist no more, after it sounds like, looks like somethin that's already been seen a million times. originality remains at the bottom of the disposal in the sink of seas.

francisco had to do the sound track ova, well some of it. so he flew in the two actors who had to redub their voices. exavier and john king. john king goes to school at howard university. he's short and round with big baby eyes and would always be sayin in a deep funny voice—somethin gonna grab you. somethin gonna jump out the bushes and grab ya.

joseph mc breed down on avalon, near watts—and his old greasy recordin studio in his own backyard was where francisco did the sound track ova. he found mc breed through chuck—a friend of francisco's who told francisco he didn't need to spend the money to get exavier and john to fly in from nowheres. that he could get two men to do their voices ova, but francisco wasn't goin for it. joseph mc breed converted his garage into a recording studio that had all facilities needed—all the facilities that any hollywood studio would have. francisco says he wasn't that good—that mc breed was always fallin asleep on the job. i became cook and such always off to the store to get beer, juices, wine, watermelon, nuts, and chicken. the redubbing was completed during one weekend. it took two hard days to redub this bus scene in spite of mc breed's lectures.

one sunday morning we got there about ten, and mc breed was waitin for us with an early mornin sermon. he was in a clean shirt, freshly pressed pants on his skinny bow-legged legs. his hair wavy oiled down to a slick shine. his bloodshot eyes as bloodshot as eva cause mc breed is a wino. mc breed talked about angela, about white folks bein the great imitators of all time, bout the whole rip off thing. he spoke in an intelligent sophisticated nigga southern rhythm. i liked him. i thought he was cute. he thought i was cute too, till we started talkin to each otha, then we would get into arguments—behind him sayin that women were put here to be controlled by men and have been fightin their natural place in life eva since the beginnin of time.

francisco lost a friend in the process—chuck—who escaped with two hundred dollars of francisco's. but that was alright i guess—cause i didn't hear about that very much i heard mostly bout how charles thought too much.

this morning the trash can was burnin, and i put the napkins in the icebox. that's better than two days before. i put the eggs in the freezer, and francisco saw it. he came in the bedroom where i lay reading a book, black manhattan by james weldon johnson, and told me quietly intensely controllin himself, not to put the eggs in the freezer please. he's trying to be cool after gettin almost angry enough to slap me around a couple of times cause he came home one day and found that i had painted the icebox, stove, heater in living room, and chest in hallway bright red.

anyways
last night we went ova to david war's house. he had a surprise party given for him by his old lady, marie davidson, a short nice white lady, that's into bein nice. marie's about thirty and well taken care of and david's just turned twenty-seven, black, looks like he's forty. francisco says david always looked old. he was born lookin old.

david had a black liberation flag hangin on his wall, and all those revolutionary black books sittin around everywhere. francisco wore a beautiful black velvet suit and his silva high heel shoes. he's cute with that mighty conquistador moustache and all. we went out and danced to stevie wonder's latest album and carried on, it's hard to dance with francisco cause all i want to do is laugh all ova. cause he dances real funky—he finished his film yesterday. this morning george eves called up and said francisco ought to marry me. i think so too. george eves is a man i met in n.y.—a friend of an x-old man of mine. george eves now works and lives in s.f. folks sure do move around. francisco wanted george to get some footage of angela out of some newsroom. george couldn't do it. francisco managed to get somebody else who worked at some otha news studio to do it—francisco got the film had it copied and returned it back to its respective place without any high up's or low in-between's knowin it had been borrowed. francisco put his arms around my sweaty waist just now my waist is sweaty cause i been exercisin.

he hugged me.

and said he loved me, and i smiled my regular full blush.

now i tell you francisco was ova editor taylor's house about a week ago. and we managed to sit ova there watchin t.v. till one in the mornin. i think we would have been there till dawn if it had been left up to francisco cause he didn't feel like movin. editor and francisco started talkin about the latest book editor has co-min out, and editor was pullin out press releases and historical facts about afro-american culture. i believe he gave me the dis-tinct impression of havin studied, researched everything about black people that was or might be magical, fantasy or real.

we met editor in the anchor bar, hangin out in berkeley cause we had driven ova there one weekend visitin francisco's par-ents ... so there we were walkin into this bar and there sits editor with five other writers from the area. francisco started talkin to editor about his book—green front t.v. fixed up which francisco wanted to direct, and is goin to direct cause editor gave the word of mouth rights to do it—and so they were sittin beatin the rug all night long about angela—crackin up on the way she talked. crackin up on how each otha talked. this sense of humor of theirs has no respect for themselves, or nothin. it is cold-blooded somehow true—just downright fracturingly factual.

one night francisco, exavier and i were ridin along be-boppin after comin from mini's can do (an old timey lookin bar where folks go to dance to old timey music, out of the forties and fifties. i played on an upright piano. they got this intermission where singas who are on their way to gettin on their way sing, and carry on).
crackin up on how
sam cooke got burnt
james brown drowned in a cold sweat
jimi hendrix got caught in a purple haze
and completin their comedy by sayin,
pardon me, but dig this. (in honor of their friend john, the weasel).

and francisco loves jimi hendrix and jimmy reed. francisco got jimi hendrix hangin off his walls and shit—he be playin jimi hendrix in the mornin for his takin a shower-music. jimi should of died in africa.

crackin up on how james brown was funkier to him when he had a konk. i think he only makes fun of people he loves. he don't botha with people he don't care about one way or the otha. he was makin fun of how editor will bring out a book to prove what he is sayin—editor will bend ova pointin to a page in a book sayin

read it. read it … it's right there!

you got to see editor, to appreciate what i mean. he's an abrupt, direct, exact grangly powerfully stout lookin mad man with light brown color i think, and a cute smile when he smiles. he's crazy too. his wife ann, who has real long hair down to her ankles i bet, always wears her hair in a bun at the back of her head. ann fixed some millet for dinna that night, and some duck. it sure was good. i was slightly drunk and very much not here. i be wanderin off sometimes—and when i come back i cannot tell you where i have been, cause i do not even know i was gone.

so at five-thirty today, we're all gonna go down to sausalito and screen the film in some screenin room for our friends and for francisco to examine it, and see if he is pleased with the new party scene, and the new sound. it's mainly for him, and then sunday we're goinna drive down to l.a. and check out hollywood. i don't know i think it's not so much behind every great man is a great woman. as much as a great man is a great man and a girl is a girl.

george eves came ova with a red scarf flying round his neck, red and white striped pants on—red shirt, under an orange sleeveless sweater, blue red yellow high heel men's shoes on, a red scarf danglin from his left wrist, and his big gorilla before mankind time hands along with his gory, scoury, pockmarked, kind, grotesque face. high on acid.

exavier and john have been gettin drunk off of beer and strawberry hill wine—talkin loud. we all have a good time. i didn't get drunk today. cause today is my off drunk day. we all drove down to sausalito—we all, included lennie and lady friend with false eyelashes and rich lookin town and country clothes on (but they got lost followin us down, and neva saw the film) and francisco's cousin, besides of course george eves, and me, and everybody else right?

we arrived to find the screenin room to be a house shack by the ocean surrounded by junk. a big junkyard full of wood and rusty parts of old crusty cars that somehow got humped up on top of each otha in front of thick woolly itchy trees and weeds that hide some steps that lead up to a rickety plank that met some wooden shaky steps that lead to the house shack where francisco's film was to be screened.

i'm tired now from bein happy, so i might not tell this right— but the house looked like it was in the appalachian hills of west virginia. it was beautiful, rustic, wooden, and old fash-ioned pictures of old timey white folks hung on the walls. we stood in the house just as the sun was goin down in orange and turquoise—those colors lit the room warmly. about four or five people were sittin on an old raggedy great lookin couch— greeted us warmly, the women didn't have any makeup on, or shoes—they looked like they were out of tobacco road with style. they were kind and offered us wine, and showed us around their house. there was this truly beautiful room that had windows so clean that you could see the ocean and sky meetin. there was a velvet antique sofa, a brass bed with an antediluvian well maintained quilted blanket on top.

i could have lived there.
it was a romantic place. especially at that time of day.
sundown.
michel cerf came with his wife who is pregnant and he brought two french people, husband and wife movie makin team who were visitin michel from hollywood for the weekend. they had to return on monday to continue work on their film. george

eves was on acid, john and exavier on wine. i was on apples
and francisco was just on.

the film started.
i must say i was nervous.
i was a nervous wreck because i love francisco and i wanted
that film to be great.
i watched the people watch the film. their eyes never left the
screen. when there were breaks (francisco had to change reels)
they didn't move but sat fixed in seats while the seas shifted
outside, waitin for the film to continue.

michel cerf whispered to francisco after each reel—(they
adore it. my friends adore it.)

when the film was ova, michel cerf invited us all ova his house,
also in sausalito. so we didn't have to drive far.

now we get in the house, exavier immediately starts hittin on
this cute round short hair cutted french girl, by pullin on his
big bodacious nose, stretchin his red liva lips sideways up and
down acting like step left to fetch it—the french woman filmmaker susan, who was a thirty-year-old woman full of life and
youth, about five-foot-two got upset and yelled in her thick
french accent—she will marry a french man! a french man!
i don't know why susan got so excited, cause the cute french
girl viewed exavier's antics in complete boredom, turning to
me once to say, oh, i've seen such antics before.

at the same time george eves asks me what am i doin with

myself? it looks like i'm just trippin, wastin time. i started walkin around with cashew nuts in my hands, poppin them into my mouth as i looked out through the slidin glass door windows to take in the streaks of passin sun light easin in through the leaves of all the trees rockin back and forth in a slow lilt to the evenin wind comin on, and the light hazel blue eyes sausalito had for a sky. but george pursued me in each step tellin me he was goin to marry me after i divorce francisco in about five years from now, when he's made it. i ain't even been proposed to by francisco yet, who sat on the couch cozy and content talkin to six-foot-nine forty-year-old, long black sprinkled grey thinnin hair raoul, susan's french enormously tall husband. susan, raoul, michel, and francisco discussed films, while michel's lovely blonde haired pregnant wife furnished her guests with enough peanuts, akadama wine, champagne, cold duck, beer, and her warm spreading smiles even while exavier straggled his ears and rolled his eyes. raoul and susan loved the way francisco edited the film, they said ova and ova in their charming french accents filled with admiration and excitement—your film is wonderful.

exavier and john got drunk. exavier grew obtuse, loud alternating from stretchin his nose to takin ova all the otha conversations carrying on a dynamited monologue as to how he was a great actor, while movin his arms, head and feet in a boxer's movement. but john sat straight faced quiet, starin into the straight ahead. pardon me, but dig this. are you happy? i heard him only because i happened to be near. his eyes wide completely transfixed still passed on to anotha state of unconsciousness, removed not even hearin anythin that was goin on around him.

michel had to carry john out when we finally did leave. exavier tumbled along on his own two feet. both were too drunk to drive, so george eves did. imagine, two drunks sittin in the front seat beside the man behind the wheel who's on acid. what a team.

i offered to drive, but francisco told me to mind my own business or go to business school.

they were suppose to follow us but we lost them on the highway.

francisco and i got home and changed our clothes in complete jubilation. again. i could have ripped his clothes right off him, and thrown him down on the bed. but we were goin to anotha party. a party ova marie's house, who francisco told me was one of his girlfriends. we got dressed up great, francisco in his velvet suit again cause i asked him to wear it and me in my long clingin white dress.

exavier and john and george arrived. exavier slightly sobered up. george eves on the case professionally—he really knows how to deal with acid.

we arrive at marie's party ova in berkeley. nothing but white folks dancing to the rollin stones. there was some good cheeses and different kinds of breads and big bottles of wine. tad, my friend the painter was there, we took a walk on the street together and talked about life and love and games. francisco changed the music and put on james brown's coldsweat. he came and got me to dance with him.

i don't dig james brown too tough. or maybe i just didn't like bein there. i mean i like parties that got some black folks there, at least ten, cause when we all get togetha sweat be pourin from the walls and shit—energy be so sizzlin hot high and i have a good time without even thinking about it. but as i danced with francisco surrounded by all those white folks i just didn't get the same feelin. so i sat down in a chair and just watched the party.

there were only two black men there, both of whom were leanin on the walls next to white women who were actin like they thought janis joplin would act maybe. a young man sat down beside me. i don't know. i felt strange cause i was happy and here i was at a party that i wanted to come to, and i had a lot to dance and feel good about because francisco's film was good—but here—there i sat—sittin in a chair discussin the difference between n.y., s.f., and l.a. with this soft-spoken shy short, long hair down to his ass rubberbanded in a ponytail, white young man.

marie turned out to be a nice girl, with long wavy blonde hair, blue eyes, she is pretty. in passin she smiled at francisco saying, i see you got yourself a black girl. it's about time. exavier was after pussy george was after me, after every otha girl, havin a good time bein after everythin. francisco danced, and came back and saw about me every now and then. i didn't want to drink no wine, so i went in the kitchen and got some apple juice out the icebox. i heard that this girl named anchor, cause she had a reputation of trying to hold to each and every man she randomly made it with, was out in the backyard with black bill, who looked like a dinosaur, doin it, on the mildewed grass.

francisco's sister was there. i had been lookin forward to meeting this thin, light-skinned, straightened haired, fine nose, stuck up small lipped girl. francisco says his sister has never been with a black man. she is twenty-three and recently divorced from a wealthy jew. francisco says some families are fucked up cause they feel they ain't white enough.

francisco and i left, and drove back to s.f. and sat at enrico's drinkin coffee and eatin cheesecake. even though we were fulfilled by his film, there was still the day to day problem of money. i had tried to get money by sellin my car, and i also tried to get three hundred dollars from my mother which she owes me, since that didn't work i asked her to send me three hundred dollars out of my trust fund which she wouldn't do because i am irresponsible, and she won't let me have it till i'm thirty. i might not live till i'm thirty, and it's my money, my labor. i worked for it, where upon she informed me as to how she helped me in my career, and i told her yeah, you helped me and i appreciate it, but i'm the one who did it, you didn't. if i redecorated the bathrooms in your house, remodeled your pool, mowed your lawn every day, and helped you pay the rent, it would still be your house. so it is with my career, with the money i made in my work. i could see you refusin me, and being totally right if i was askin you to give me some of your money, some money you worked for. then you could make some judgments but not with mine. legally it's mine. but she knows i ain't got the money, the wherewithal to take her to court. besides she's all the way down in west virginia, besides i don't want to take her to court. i know she feels she's lookin out for me, but—

i'm unimpressed by effort. in this world what you try or tried to do, don't count. nobody cares about what you could of done. it's what you did, what you do that counts, francisco said.

my momma probably knows about francisco via my dad, and probably felt it was for francisco, and she's afraid that i will be used, and exploited, and—but you can't tell a parent about how you believe in someone, how you want to help them, see them accomplish what they want to accomplish, you can't tell a parent about how you have faith, how you're willin to love an alive life.

francisco was silent. i was silent with him for a long time. starin at the cars goin by, the people passin by. some of the women francisco knew. i thought everythin was perfect in the film cept for the beginnin. i felt it needed to be cut somehow. i felt strange about openin my mouth to say that, but i opened my mouth and said it anyway. he listened.

we got home about two or three, and fell asleep. it had been a good day.

the next day francisco called me into his bedroom and showed me the first ten minutes of the film on that little cardboard screen. he asked me what i thought needed to be cut. i showed him the places, and suggested ideas. we edited the film to-getha. then francisco continued on his own, cause him and me disagreed somewheres about somethin.

now it's sunday. and i got this little black cat from david war's house this morning. francisco and i got up out of bed early, and walked up three steep hills to david's house—and got some waffles, sausage, and conversation. david said all in the family was great that its humor was comparable to amos and andy. i didn't see no comparison at all, i've never watched all in the family that much, but i don't have to to know there ain't no comparison at all. i use to hurry myself home everyday after school in junior high to see amos and andy, and the little rascals.

but one time in a chinese restaurant the manager of some black comedienne's clothes told me that he felt the show (all in the family) was great cause by makin fun of bigotry one decreased its powa.

francisco didn't want me to have this kitten, and it's been squawking. francisco says some of my ideas make him sick. he later got angry at me cause he was tired and asked me to leave for a while and give him some peace. i took the cat back. i'm glad cause i think it would have been terrible drivin from s.f. to l.a. with that sweet little kitten cause francisco's head is real sensitive, and irritable now all hung up on his film.

so much has happened since i last sat down to really write somethin. i wrote a couple of days ago when i was sittin on the beach—the first day at chris's house with francisco and exavier. exavier flew in from s.f. about a day or two afta francisco and i drove to l.a.

we had a nice ride talkin bout who we'd like to fuck that's famous. we started out with black folks. francisco couldn't think of any black woman famous he'd like to fuck besides of course marpessa dawn. i couldn't think of no black famous man i wanted to fuck. once i wanted to fuck huey newton when i was sixteen, but not no more.

francisco could think of plenty of white women he wanted to fuck. his list did not include elizabeth taylor or brigitte bardot. he likes claudia cardinale. i couldn't think of nobody. as a last resort i said maybe ralph nader.

we talked about revolutionists. i hate revolutionists. i'm tired of all that who shot john. they all turn out to be movie stars in this country anyway. or the government puts them in jail and fucks with their brains through some drugs producing chemical changes then releases them when they can't see straight no more. seems like most of the breakthroughs have been broken up. seems like almost everybody has been bought.

we decided revolutionists are somebody—anybody who does somethin true in this world—free from being held back by the manipulative powa money established controlling, deciding, structures at present. in terms of films, black films—we decided that sweetback bad ass song was a revolutionary film in that it was a true success financially for melvin van peebles, and the most original film out there.

anyway in my egotistical fantasy i was talkin bout if i eva got famous people would have to hear about me to see me. i'd be too busy doin what i do to talk about it.

francisco laughed at me like i was crazy. i would, i'd be cookin and scrubbin down them walls, and watchin my kids' nappy-headed uncombed hair grow, and singin and swimmin in a lake somewhere naked, and having parties and gettin up, after gettin down, and i'm from egypt. i feel i lived in egypt. i am egyptian. francisco believes me.

exavier rented some kind of american car. he had to have a credit card to rent it. green money crisp and real wouldn't rent a car. it don't make no sense to me how money won't even rent a car in this bureaucratic jail. i mean ain't money suppose to be the standard form of exchange? i mean ain't money suppose to buy everythin? ain't it? first they tie you up by makin you got to work factory hours day in day out just to get by. then they tie you up forcin folks to get credit cards. i mean what is this?

anyway, exavier and francisco hung out at the lab at consolidated film industries for a couple of days workin. i didn't see much of them cept when exavier slept on the couch in the den and asked me for a pillow, and i only saw francisco when he slept in what use to be the maid's room, but became my room, cause we neva did have no maid—he asked me for an extra blanket.

francisco used to sneak and sleep in my bedroom with me, my father never found out. i have twin beds in my bedroom and francisco slept in one, me in the otha. my father would get up and go to work without eva knowin that francisco had slept in my room. it didn't matter. we neva did nothin no way.

chris called me, and told me she was going to n.y. with her old man. i asked if i could stay in her pad while she was gone, cause i wanted to get out of my house with exavier and francisco before my dad put me out—and besides, i just wanted to stay there. chris had just moved out to malibu.

Part II

Living Off the Land

Malibu.
(Muscle Beach, Annette Funicello, and Fabian, yeah, yeah, yeah.)

it's nice here.
the first day i got here i walked out on the beach alone, took off
all my clothes and faced my fear of the raging black ocean, and
soaked myself in its madness. the ocean is an old friend. the
first day i felt strange cause everybody got blonde hair around
these parts. i mean everybody.

i sat on the beach the second day. some young blonde eyed
freckled face innocent little animals came ova and talked to
me. they found some birds and showed them to me. little baby
birds they stole from a nest, and put in a box—they were all
excited cause their momma said they could keep them.

one tiny little girl about four wandered ova to my legs sat on
my lap, searched my face closely. she pointed to the dots on
my face.
what are those? she asked.
freckles, i answered.
where'd you get them?
from god.

oh ... (she paused curiously) does he have any more?
i don't know ... why?
i want some ... i want some like yours.

i broke out gigglin softly as she went on talkin—tellin me that
her name was cheyenne, and she was "these many"—holdin
up four fingers, "years old." then one of the older boys, bill—
who was round and twelve and pimpled face instead of freckled who had been talkin bout his dad bein a policeman, how
kids talked bad about him cause his dad was a policeman who
worked in governor reagan's buildin got stung by a jellyfish
and judy went and got some ammonia to put on his sting.

marnicke, the oldest girl, about thirteen told me that if the
folks around here didn't have naturally blonde hair, they dyed
it or bleached it to make sure they did. then she took cheyenne into their house two houses down from chris's. cheyenne
kissed me goodbye, and said in her tiny sweet angel voice, we
love ... we love. marnicke held cheyenne's hand to keep her
from tumblin as they walked along the beach—cheyenne
turnin around every now and then wavin bright smilin good-
byes. soon judy, bill, and the rest of the kids followed.

francisco and exavier are up in the house watchin t.v. or just
talkin. once i was up there and they were talkin about magic.

the ocean and sun feels good. i guess he loves me. i really don't
know. (here i go digressing again—here i go loop-t-loop.) occasionally he's very cold to me—distant. at first it upset me
but i am learnin for it not to. i think of nothin but francisco's
success, our love. i am not afraid. i only want to be with fran-

cisco. i'd marry him. i'm crazy i guess. i don't like the way he sneaks and reads shit that ain't none of his business. i don't like the way he wears the same underwear day afta day but i'd marry him anyway.

then the kids came back. i was sittin and writin. the kids asked me what i was writin. a letter? to whom? i don't know yet. i was amused by their lack of self-consciousness. i asked judy what did her fatha do.

aw he's dead now but he used to work at mcdonnell douglas, a scientific firm.

that's where my father works. he a radio-chemist. he used to run track in college. exavier, francisco, and i had a suppose to be conversation that turned into an argument as to what took more concentration—to be a bullfighter or a track runner. me and francisco said bullfighter, exavier said track runner.

exavier is gettin cross upset and hostile. exavier couldn't get no woman. so he flew in delilah from alabama. and i noticed exavier's attitude cooled out, and he started actin like he had some sense.

delilah.
she's a tall black indian cheekboned lanky woman girl. i like her. she dresses like she reads essence magazine or vogue. she got sophisticated nine to five taste. she's nice, she got a son about four years old in alabama. she's been married. exavier got rid of her after two days. exavier, francisco, and i went out to dinna. where upon exavier started gettin on my case about how

i acted stuck up or somethin. how i'm not the finest woman in the world. (i never said i was.) and talkin about how francisco goes to parties and he wants to fuck every girl in sight. francisco just ignored him. i wish exavier would go back to s.f. i like him and stuff. but i think he's sick of me, and it's hard to be around folks when they're sick of you. besides his wife keeps callin up here askin for exavier. exavier's wife works at some job and makes twenty-thousand a year i assume, and tells me exavier neva supported her or the children since they've been married, exavier has three lovely sons he loves very much.

francisco told me about the times he lived in africa. how it changed his whole life. it was in africa that he realized he wanted to be a filmmaker. his original goal was to be a lawyer. he started sex late in his life. in africa he remembers bein out in the bush and how a jeep broke down, and tribesmen who knew nothin about the workins of a car, searched through the hood, took out a little piece of metal, broke a branch from a nearby tree, and cut it up, shaved it down until it duplicated the metal, put the wooden duplicate in its place, and the jeep worked.

he says a woman is a luxury, somethin i don't need. i mean personal relationships usually end up in tragedy and i usually shy away from gettin involved. in the past, i've given as little as possible—the bare minimum. that always was enough.

then he said he was gonna write a book about me and call it, return of the fish market, cause my pussy smells like fish. i mean he said it smelled like guppies, and crabs, lobsters, tadpoles, and everythin down there. oh. i said, not knowin how to take that. maybe i should use some of the lady stuff they make for down there. francisco laughed and pulled me to him. no, he smiled, addin on the sly, i like all that funkiness don't be puttin no chemicals down there and destroy the real thang.

the subject changed to birth control pills and how there's this train of thought that niggas shouldn't take no contraceptives cause that intent was genocide. niggas should have as many babies as possible to give growth to a majority creatin a powerful race. francisco said that didn't make no sense, proven so by the example in south africa—where the majority is ruled by the minority. quantity is alright, but the goal should be to develop a strong race of quality. then i started talkin bout how i didn't think no woman needed to take those pills. that a woman can control pregnancy in her mind.

i fixed tea, put some wine in it, made tuna fish sandwiches while i was telling francisco when i was twelve i was real tall, as tall as i am and skinny—i had the skinniest legs—and i started prayin every night for big legs, and now i got them, see? one time i told this marvelous, round-faced great man friend of mine, d'urville, that same story and he looked me straight in the eyes and said well, that goes to prove a person can pray too much. francisco fell out laughin then told me yeah—he prayed to be six-foot-two, cause see he was short most of his teenage and adult life. he prayed to be exactly six-foot-two, and now he's six-foot-two.

then i started talkin bout how i thought america was the wizard of oz country. i think a million times a little puppy pulls back the curtain and finds a scared weak snifflin man playin with some big toy—but that big toy ain't no joke cause it affects people's lives, controls people's lives, destroys peoples lives. hush francisco said. i closed my mouth and opened it only to sip tea, wine, and bite into the sandwich.

i always wanted to go ova to mc breed's and make a demo of my music to send to someone to hear, so that maybe they will produce it, but you know sometimes i just like bein with francisco. i forget about my music—i forget about myself sometimes. i know that's not good but it happens to me sometimes. i'm gonna change. i'll have to, cause my music haunts me and i'll have to get it out. i played my music one night at mini's can do in s.f. before i sat down at the piano bench before my fingers hit that beautiful upright piano the folks applauded. i blushed, then lifted my head up into a smile, opened my mouth, and sang, playin off. francisco was there in the audience. i like just playin for friends, for folks you know. i don't always feel like i got to get out there to make a record and carry on. but i sure did love playin that night at mini's can do. i sure did love singin for those people while they drank beer and wine, and i sure did love seein francisco's smile prevail through the room, bouncin off the walls. i had stopped playin for a while. i mean i have a piano in my father's house, but i hadn't touched it for six months, cause i was hurtin from some of the experiences i had had before tryin to do an album. i went down to mc breed's to record, howeva he wasn't there.

we watched t.v. and lay on the beach. carol asked us ova to drink some wine. francisco went ova and sat up and entertained them with his jokes. i went inside chris's house for a while, and then went ova to carol's and listened to the roaring laughta of carol, this overweight pink man bulgin out of his bikini bathin suit, and a sweet girl with long blonde hair.

carol is in her thirties—her body firm and taken care of. her hair dyed bleached blonde black rooted. she wanted to fuck francisco—she came ova here lookin for him one night when he and i were gone to the city. francisco said she had buck teeth, too old, too ugly. she has a t.v. show that she interviews people on—she told exavier to tell francisco she wanted him to be on her show. francisco laughed upon hearin that piece of news. i asked him if he would fuck her. he said he might let her suck his toes.

yeah, so we stayed in the beach house and listened to james brown's cold sweat, we found it as i was searchin through chris's records, trying to figure out what to listen to. chris knows what's happenin. we listened to james brown's cold sweat ova and ova. i've neva been into james brown. i saw him once on ed sullivan years ago when he had his konk gleamin in fried grease and he did please, please please—fallin all ova, caressin the microphone. i thought that was great. but i wouldn't have gone to see him or nothin. he just didn't move me thataway. i never bought none of his records. neva. francisco said he would take me to see him the next time he played somewhere. james brown got this great funkiness that started hittin me right in the gut of rhythm. francisco lay on the sofa, and i sat stretched out on the chair loose relaxed lettin the music permeate my body—slide up my legs wide open—free. we listened to that cold sweat ova and ova … curtains in the living room were closed, but we could hear the beat of ocean waves joinin in.

i couldn't see francisco from where i was sittin cause i was sittin straightways and he was sittin sideways on the sofa, he'd have to lift up to see my face cause the chair was higha than the sofa. at best just layin down without movin. all he could see was my legs and feet. and i couldn't see him less i turned my head sideways. but i could feel him. i mean sometimes we laughed at the same exact time/place as we listened to our man sing his song, and grunt. see james brown makes francisco laugh, and feel good. and me too now. all we listened to all night long was: break out! in a c – o – l – d sweat!

i got in tune with francisco's pace, which was slow and light and easy, my spirit in peaceful union with francisco's. there we sat, two out of it niggas — the room we sat in, the record playa turnin round and round — ocean waves comin in and goin out — everythin was in union with us. we fumed without touchin. i felt francisco's rhythm. i experienced an exchange with a man that night, that i've neva experienced before. i felt sensual and peaceful and slow and could feel myself unwindin from anotha state i usually function in. i left francisco in the living room at about six in the mornin (afta openin the curtains to see the sun rise). i fell asleep on the bed in my clothes.

chris is comin back tomorrow with her old man, dave. editor taylor called and told francisco sam revels wants to make a film out of his book too, and francisco has to get two thousand dollars to buy the option. francisco found out he has four hundred dollars left in the bank. he got his film out of the lab today, and will start showin it to distributors next week. he wants to direct green front in africa, and figures it will cost half million dollars. he says that's not a lot. francisco calls me his old lady now.

did i ever tell you the outside of francisco's old s.f. antediluvian

house is painted red, not bright red though. kind of a burnt
red, and the house right across the street is a psychedelic lime
green.

at one in the morning dave came and peeped his head through
his bedroom door and found me and francisco in arms huggin
each otha—francisco and i had just come back from carol's
house next door.

see francisco and i had been somewhere in the city havin a
good time and even though chris had called to say she'd be
back, she had been callin for the last three days sayin she'd be
back, so i really didn't think she'd show. so francisco and i came
back to malibu instead of movin back in my fatha's house.

carol drove up at the same time francisco and i were headed
down the steps to our gift house. friendly and all she grinned
and invited us ova to her house for a drink. we went. she had
a guy ova sittin on her plastic pillows, who offered francisco
advice about how distributors will rip you off man, and that's
how it is. francisco said the point is to talk about how you're
not gonna get ripped off—the ways it can be prevented. carol
was okay i told her i saw her on her t.v. show, and it was a nice
show. she asked me if as an actress could i offa her a positive critique. i told her i thought she could comb her hair back so folks
could see her face. cause her bangs were monstrous. i mean she
looked alright in life like that, but i think she did herself an in-
justice with all them bangs hangin all over her eyebrows.
so i sipped wine,
watched smoke circle in the air, while francisco drank beer.
imagine. he don't hardly even drink. he's neva taken acid. he

don't even take vitamins. he is totally natural. i mean i haven't met anyone like that in years still walkin around. you figure everybody in america is on some kind of pills or somethin— they be advertising pills on t.v. for kids and shit, pills to put folks to sleep and shit. we split from carol's house biddin her and her guest a good night. we walked arm in arm to our malibu hideaway. the ocean's night roarin strong like a lion. francisco and i went in the den and watched t.v. i left him on the den couch afta a while. i got tired and went to bed. francisco turned off the t.v. some time lata. i listened to him walk through the house turning off the lights, makin sure the doors were locked. my body temperature risin as i listened to him walk from room to room. he came in the bedroom and shut the door. he undressed in the dark. we made love.

i rested in his arms, almost fallin asleep to our whispered conversation when i saw this baldheaded face peep through the door quickly observin in shock-eyes covered by a pair of spectacles. dave. oh lord. they're here! what mess.

dave closed the door. i popped up. they're here i giggled. i mean i was feelin so good you know, and here we were two niggas layin in a jewish man's bed. francisco told me to shut up.

chris came rushin in, no makeup on her eyes, lookin great without it, and a new silk pants suit on her small lithe body dave bought her in n.y.

dave's fumin.
francisco split to the den with a blanket while i moved all our suitcases and paraphernalia to the den so we could depart in

the morning at chris's request with our belongings. francisco was pissed. dave was pissed. dave just got off the airplane and was tired, didn't expect us to be there and didn't like it. francisco was pissed cause he felt dave's attitude was makin a big deal out of nothin. if he had been the host he wouldn't of made the people get out the bed at one in the mornin. he said there were plenty of beds around here. he felt it was some kind of a jewish superiority trip.

well i fell asleep on the den couch with francisco—we woke up and got dressed then departed. chris left me a note on the kitchen counter. she said she had stayed up all night practically unable to sleep due to some diet pill and also because she was upset with dave, though she understood how he felt. it was a nice note. she had read the beginnings of some poetry i was writin, and mentioned that she liked it. she said we should get togetha and write a screenplay. she also asked about a silk dress that had been thrown in a hamper with a soppin wet towel. who did that?

francisco and i got in his blue volks car, and drove along pacific coast highway, our lost weekend begun—we stopped at al's rancho restaurant on the highway and had some toast and tea. we didn't have no money—so here we were stuck with a weekend, no dough, no sure place to stay cause i wasn't sure how my father was gonna act when we showed up at his door. so francisco would have to go into his sneakin thing again and neither one of us looked forward to that, cause in short we were just tired of stayin at people's houses though we were blessed. we gathered our dimes and quartas togetha discoverin that we did have at least four or five dollars. lord, i felt rich.

we wasted some of it in the restaurant as i looked out on the ocean below. a black man was out bright and early with hooks and all fishin at peace with a straw hat topped to the side of his head. the jukebox played timely notables that i wiggled my body to. we sat and chuckled bout what i can't rememba. mainly how the evening would have gone if he was the host of dave's house. i mainly looked out at the ocean, enjoyin the fact that i had finally gotten fucked afta bein at malibu for almost two weeks, taken birth control pills at this man's requests, and him completely into some kiss me tight, hug me at night routine that had me wonderin if he had lost sexual interest in me, or would i have to go and get it from somewhere else before i turned into a soppin wet neurotic bitch. francisco noticed i was unusually bright and cheerful for someone who had had to get out of a big bed early in the morning, and leave one gypsy camp for anotha ... yeah, i was happy.

the weekend turned out to be cool. we sat up and watched t.v. at my father's house, after my father told me i should go to college and do somethin with my life.

francisco made me and him a buttered juicy corn, fried fish with a dab of wheat germ on it, thick crisp french fries dinna. we offered my dad some, he took some french fries in his hands, and ate that, that was about all, being casual cool aloof.

and then at my father's request we helped him scrub down the kitchen with him and this lady friend of his, rochelle.

rochelle was talkin bout how she didn't dig on muhammad ali cause he had a whole organization behind him, or somethin

like that. to me, that don't make no sense. it's great that he
has a whole organization to support him, if they do. i mean
i wouldn't want to hear about him going crazy like joe louis
bein takin advantage of monetarily by his manager endin up,
sittin up in some bar in las vegas as some kind of figurehead.
or being ripped off like jimi hendrix was who should have
lived a long life and died in africa instead of cold stone lon-
don town, and francisco got a telephone call from a person
wishin to remain unknown informin him that a major motion
picture company here in hollywood is makin a movie rippin
off some exact scenes from editor's book, and rochelle is goin
on, about how she don't like muhammad's brand of comedy
as if that matters in the schemes of things, she don't like the
way he carries on, and look how he acted the last time. the
last time is the last time. i mean she's reactin the way the
general public stupidly reacts to an x-convict when they get
out of prison. there's a difference between confidence and
over-confidence but muhammad learned his lesson. i mean
he dealt with himself. i wish the revolution had taken place.
that's why everythin is wishy-washy like it is. you got to make
a stand, now, here foreva. you can't be talkin about no may-
bes. nothin will eva change that way but the weather. francisco said muhammad looked good, like in the old days. he
sat up and watched him on t.v. fight jerry quarry. my dad just
listened enjoyin the argument. see my dad's a quiet dude —
a heart hard workin dude. he smokes a pipe and looks real
distinguished when he gets ready to, and digs dark-skinned
black women, but all women dig my dad. most of the time
around the house he wears old clothes, raggedly tennis shoes,
and a huge mexican hat that he got in mexico years ago, when
he took the family down there one summa vacation when the

family was young. i think anna had just graduated from high school.

anna use to make straight A's in high school, mainly cause she worked double hard for them cause white teachas just didn't give a nigga an A cause a nigga just simply might have deserved it. anna would come home crying sometime when she got a A-minus, or a B-plus, because she worked hard for an A and didn't get it. mom always went right up to the school and talked to the teacher, or whomever she had to talk to so anna could get the grade she deserved. funny, how they always gave the african exchange students A's easy. see anna went to a mostly jewish white school with a spatterin of just recently released from california concentration camp quiet japanese americans, who pretty much stuck togetha. they're smart. it would be somethin incredible to see how things would change, if niggas stuck togetha. i mean half the changes we go through workin to get somethin done would be obsolete.

but dad was happy with the two of us young folks in the kitchen—he was just a smilin. it's nice to see him smilin so, he doesn't smile very often these days.

so there we were all just a talkin and carryin on with rochelle who would have her way. i didn't press the point too much after i said, ain't nothin wrong with havin the support of a whole organization behind you. that's great. everybody needs some kind of support behind him. get the support of the whole world.

but i realized i was talkin to an adult who felt she should be right just because she had lived longa, and besides what did i know? i was walkin around callin muhammad ali muhammad ali when his momma named his cassius clay. (when movie stars change their name, i ain't heard no one refuse to call them the acquired movie star name.) and how she felt that joe louis was a natural talent, and muhammad ali had developed his skills.

i remembered when i was in madison square garden watchin him fight that australian a couple of years ago. i can't rememba the australian's name at the moment, but i rememba how much i wanted muhammad to win.

i had caught this subway and he happened to be on that very same subway with bundini and several other men surroundin him. i just got in there with them and followed them along to madison square garden and asked ali if he could get me in. he called me the wild one, and told me to just stick with him, and i did. and saw my man win. later after the fight, i heard where he was stayin and went over to the hotel. the guard at the gate wouldn't let me through and i saw ali and called him. he turned around and told the guard to let me through — that i was his friend.

there was a small party goin on in his room on the fourth floor somewhere, and i went on through and sat on the floor next to his round faced dark reddish brown haired, soft spoken mother. ali was pretty broken up that night, scarred all ova his face. but you know he sat down in a chair after fightin after doing his life work and talked to a whole bunch of young black kids out in the hallway. he didn't have to do that, but he did. i mean he was just plain beautiful. i asked his mother if she was nervous for her son watchin him up there in the ring, she smiled and shook her head yes.

i went home that night feeling so good. so proud. so great. i mean when he won in madison square garden, i felt so much a part of my people—somethin spiritual and inspirational for me to go and do—to just simply want to stay alive period.

the only time i saw muhammad ali again was a year later at a play on broadway. melvin van peeble's play, ain't suppose to die a natural death, a play that the critics tried to destroy but couldn't. i saw him sittin beside his wife, as all these young girls and guys crowded around him gigglin you know.

my dad offered francisco some beer. i guess my dad figures me and francisco get down by now.

the two of them started talkin to each otha. i mean dad and francisco would see each otha and the most they would say was a withdrawn hello. not even a how are you? but dad got us playin cards with him now, and later we progressed to playin poka with pennies. a real charmer that old man is. i mean my dad can be nice when he feels like it—but usually as soon as he hits the front door he starts screamin on me bout somethin i have done wrong. and i do a lot wrong around the house cause i ain't quite housebroken. no that's a lie. i am not all that bad. i do leave the bathroom light on. i do leave my clothes in bundles all over my bedroom floor and half hangin in the closet. i do leave the curtains open, that's just cause i like sun but my dad don't like it cause he thinks people are goin to peep through the window.

but one day i was in the kitchen, it was about five-thirty and i was throwin some kind of food togetha to eat—dad came home closed the front door behind him—came in the kitchen and kissed me on the cheek. i was slightly embarrassed. i felt kind of sweet and silly inside. i haven't lived at home for a long time, so i'm gettin to know my dad again. it's nice. it is. (parents have dreams too.)

Part III

Images, Instead of Real Things, Made by the Money Mirage

as he unlaces your boots, and reaches up your skirt to take off your pantyhose, he says with tongue hangin out of one corner of his mouth loosely wet and ready, you see my purpose in life is to get people to relax.

everybody in the room laughs as you lay your head down on the bed and me drinkin champagne out of a beer bottle cracks up as i gaze through the window in this sunset boulevard in-crowd hotel room 409, lookin at the enormous poster across the street outside, introducin a new star with red lipstick on his lips, red rouge on his cheeks, red fingernail polish on his fingernails, face in emaciated profile, and his long blond hair painted to look as if it is blowin splendidly in the wind and it starts rainin outside, our order of beer, champagne, baked halibut, chiffon pie, and a chef's salad arrives, someone purringly opens the door (a woman i guess) for the mexican dressed in red jacket, white shirt, black tie, pants, and shoes ... you want a beer? i ask him.
shyly he shakes his head no.
here take a beer.
afraid to take it, he takes it, while the famous man pays the bill and gives the bellboy a huge tip.

your skirt, panties, bra and earings off, laying flat on the bed, feet stretched up in the air wide open. the famous man gazes at you warmly, what kind of hair do you have. may i take off your wig?

i started thinkin about one time when i was in s.f. in francisco's kitchen with windows that looked out on the backsteps of apartment houses in the next block and yard—and the sky kept shiftin from grey to bright sunned blue. anotha morning tryin to make up its mind.

i was walking around with my hair uncombed, cleaning up again after a good breakfast. i mean i finally got breakfast down to a science man and this nigga—this short, brown, european accented-slurrin talkin getting on his forties, sophisticated suave, fine nigga named john davis marshall—refugee from the beatnik generation—been around the world photographer, poet screenwriter, stood in the kitchen and said he disliked black women.

because all the mailmen, garbage can collectors, and half of the black men in jail are there because of black women, grinningly he sneered.

well i had to turn around and stop washin the dishes for one hot second. i think, i said very quietly, you are confusin the issue, the source, and the cause.

black women, he went on deeply disturbed—DESTROY THE DREAMS of black men; you—your sistas are the cause for the black man's loss of his staff of life. i don't want to call no woman i'm gonna love my sista. this whole syndrome of callin the black man brotha, and black woman sista is destructive to the whole sexual life between men and women ... john took one last sip of a cup of coffee and then dumped the cup in the sink splashin dishwater up in my face, while addin that black women get fat. black women don't take care of themselves. black women are the cause of the black faggot with her domineering paws.

cooly i turned to face john and found him in a rage as i said oh so now you're blamin black women for homosexuality? you and your miseducation and mental infestation of the ways of white culture based on the acquisition of the mink coat for the white woman. it's not black women you dislike it's yourself, your self-hatred. perhaps you have neva seen a white garbage can collector, or mailman, or a white wino lately, and i question your attitude toward blue collar workers — as if they were demeanin, unself respectin forms of work.

bored with the discussion, but havin not thought of a way to get rid of this man without bein rude i stayed in the kitchen and washed the pots.

maybe he said. but he sure as hell ain't seen many asian ones. well, maybe they got the good sense to believe in themselves, take care and trust their own. maybe the white man hasn't successfully infiltrated their sense of identity with self-hatred.

they have their own culture. john marshall davis screamed. oh, and the black woman took our culture away?

john was silent, grinnin at me again only this time it was deeper-grating cynical grin peerin through me in pleasure. i was glad francisco was in his bedroom editin his film, some-where near.

black women don't got no money. what can a black woman do to help a man, nothin—not a damn thing—always searchin for the pedestal of miss ann.

i laughed. there isn't a black woman who can't rememba some-where inside her, that once she was recognized as a queen. i stood on a corner and acted like a blind crazy person with a tin cup, i pawned a typewriter, and wanted to get a job nine to five, but francisco wants me to get an actin job, i went around and collected three hundred dollars. what can a black woman give a black man? she ain't got nothin to give. (many a black woman worked and put a black man through college) black women are strong, john marshall davis proclaimed as if that statement was meant to be an insult. oh, are you votin for weakness this year? we're suppose to be weak, is that it?

you get upset every time you see a black man with a white woman.
i yawned.
you know what upsets me. workin to live positively.

john was taken somewhat off guard. he stuttered as he regained his main line of thought, findin words, he erupted like a lion.

black men have to leave their women if they're black so they can go out in the world and pursue their dreams. you stand there and blame the pressures of life, family life on the woman. i think, john, the blame if and since you seem to be in the blamin business should be toward the white man and the way he has society stacked up. life shouldn't be as hard as it is no way. there's no reason in this world why families, why people should have to struggle and suffa as much as we do in these so-called modern times. much if not most of the human struggles we experience are scientifically, technically obsolete. there's no reason why no person shouldn't have enough clothes, and a decent place to live, that should come as natural as lovin some-body, or going to sleep at night, or wheneva a person decides to fuckin go to sleep. i mean who is to say, that the works of past generations are to be ignored, and we got to live through, go through the same fuckin shit. who is to say that i got to be forced to deal with this backwards shit because we, as people live in a country a world that's so fuckin insecure, and unwillin to allow the people to benefit from the inventions of the times we live in.

don't you see it's still the master separatin and disintegratin black family life—family life, and we allow them to. don't you see that you are admittin to bein nothin more than a modern day slave—standin on the block naked bein sold to the high-est bidder. only this time you stand up here willingly (in this kitchen) tellin me you want to be a slave.

a white woman knows how to love.

is the world the way it is because of the white man alone? is wealth uneven just because the white man is greedy? the white woman is greedy with him. a woman who knows how to love knows somethin about anotha woman's love for her man and child. and if you call knowin how to love watchin a woman thousands of women bein torn from their children, separated from their husbands, and sold. if you call knowin how to love watchin children die at the whim of her white mate—or watchin a man used for the total benefit of her family's welfare, instead of the benefit of his own family that don't probably exist no more walkin around smiling in a white frilly hat—if that is your definition of KNOWIN HOW TO LOVE then i have nothin more to say.

so now, it's in fashion to be a black woman. john smiled demurely.

unfortunately. i don't recognize the need to be in fashion. i do not need the white culture to approve my beauty, in order for me to feel some validity to my existence as a human bein, woman or black woman. that is an illusion that will not pacify me. i can not be pacified by no white condescension. the white man cannot give my life sudden acceptance, or glorification by puttin me or somebody like me on the cover of some magazine wearin some high fashion clothes, or african clothes. i existed before the media pretended to discover me. black people existed before black people discovered themselves. my beauty existed before the white man commercialized it, or bought it, and it will exist long after the black man has woken up out this western nightmare.

john marshall davis laughed hysterically. i was thinkin about goin to the laundry mat up the street, so i could wash some of them sheets, and francisco's stinky underwear. once a man told me somethin i had never heard before. he said the beauty of the black race stuns the white man. (john marshall davis by this time doubled over holdin his stomach as he laughed outrageously.) he said that the white man cannot even look at

the black man. he couldn't deal with it. that's why he made us
think we were ugly. and anythin the white man cannot deal
with frightens him—and he either destroys it or if he sees
he can make some money, some profit he usurps, he uses, he
misuses . . . he took our religion away because it scared the life
out of him. john, really, i don't feel like wastin no more of my
morning talkin bout white people.

you hate white people.

no, i don't hate no white people. i don't got time or energy to
waste hatin white folks. they don't deserve my hate. no i don't
hate no white man, i ain't in all that.

aren't you a black woman? john asked as if i had forgotten
somethin.

as i wiped my hands on my jeans, and looked ova the kitchen
to see, yeah, everythin is in place, i said clearly out of the blue,

men love women. women are beautiful if they're women.

you can't escape it . . . he yelled after me as i walked out of the
kitchen, down the hallway.

seems to me you're the one tryin to escape.

i opened the bathroom door.

there are a few things i can escape. a few things i can't and there
are a few things that escape me. excuse me please.

i shut the bathroom door behind me.

Black Women Are Strong?

i sat on the toilet in the bathroom—i've sat many a place with francisco, or by myself or just sittin talkin to chris, or havin good time passin time like watchin a kid, or feelin me wantin a kid inside of me, now in this time of supreme unpracticality. life is blunt. and so is success. failure goes round and round foreva if you don't watch out. i shall rest. i shall rest from black people. i shall snooze. i shall breathe and not see the sight of white people. i shall fly. i shall fly into the pastel colored smudged on my fingertips from paintin too many dreams on canvas, but i shall hang them up so that they may be real. people dance, forget the decay of limpin love, only rememberin that we are human and conjurin up the will to be strong, to be good. children shall come of their own accord. lovas will leave each otha to love foreva, and if i am patient i will learn to wait and know when to fight.
so i can dance, and sing all night long (decisioned pain, left out to dry. Only today there is no sun) to fulfill the capitalistic theory of girl (based on what i wear) what's the difference, if i dress up pretty, i'm the same girl. knock on wood. but he doesn't know that. modern day dilemma give me an enema. my image needs to be hospitalized. and put to rest. the doctors too embarrassed to inform me of the results of my tests. the diagram shows. enjoy youth, don't endure it. the old wino lady with no teeth said as i passed down the street. saw myself in the reflection of a store window and laughed.
i mean how could he forget his own self. how could he forget about black people bein strong. about black men bein strong

in order to survive in this madness. how could he forget that we are all victims in this madness. (watch your dreams.)

my mother told me about her father who worked as a porta in a hotel in west virginia all his life. at the end of every month the manager would call my granddad up to his office, and sittin behind a rich mahogany desk would pull a long shinin knife out from the top drawer, and say jump nigger jump. my mother said her father jumped. after he jumped the manager would hand him his pay. with the pay and tips granddad made he took care of his wife and four children. each child had a pair of school shoes, one pair of sunday shoes. sunday shoes were only worn to church or special occasions. sometimes my mother and her three brothers would sneak and wear the sunday shoes to school, but my momma's momma always caught them before they snuck out the house ... mom had two dresses. two fine dresses. her mom would wash and iron and starch them every otha night. mom always looked well taken care of she said. they didn't have much, but everythin was the best. mom always says poverty is in the mind. yeah, some folks would call my granddad an uncle tom just like folks call black people who smiled and danced in order to survive uncle toms.

i do not believe all that grinnin was weakness. i am positive some of it was a strength a magic all its own, a genius within our race. for we multiplied, we didn't use the gun all the time, but we did if we had to, sometimes we played a part. i can't figure out all this mess, all i know is i cannot deny the places from which i come. i accept them, and try to learn, grow and expand myself further. no repeat performances, shouldn't no nigga have to sing and dance again—that's already been done.

it is only for us to know what we want, and go and get it. we all struggle to get where we are or were—whetha it be considered up or down, in between, nowhere—any point has a fight all its own. now that don't mean that the fight we might be fightin at a particular time is worth it.

my mom wanted to go to college. so her dad saved his money some kind of way so she could. and when i was growin up in l.a., walkin around in my momma's high heels before they implemented black history in school, after the watts riot and every otha force that created some change, progress, sense of self awareness, my mom would sit me, my brothers (i have two brothers: one is twenty-seven and lives in europe, and don't think about comin back to this country; the other is tall, beautiful, fine, seventeen, and in jail for supposedly killin a cop), and sister down and read black poetry to us, some langston hughes, paul laurence dunbar, and give us pride in black spirituals and tell us that she thought porgy and bess was derived from our music but white folks made the fortune out of it, as usual. yeah, that ain't no big thing right, but it was for me, cause words have powa, and kids laughed in school when they saw africans on the screen, and when i would try for a part in the actin profession dependin upon the time i was just right, or not black enough, and my father's father told me once in his pompous youth when i made some statement bout how i didn't believe in tips, lookin me straight in the eyes with his straight haired high yeller white lookin self, i sent your father to college from tips.

he didn't have to say no more.

john marshall davis forgot about black men bein strong. perhaps his father left him when he was young, or was a wino, or somethin. i don't know. and maybe his mother did rule the roost. somebody had to do somethin for him while his father went off to do whateva it was he felt he had to do.

i don't know, but i know there are many alternative examples in the history of my people, and just because somethin is a reality doesn't mean that it should be accepted, doesn't mean that it can't be changed, and doesn't mean that it's right.

Part IV

It All Started With Momma's Supa-Eight

Lost Weekend Found.

we drank sodas up on sunset boulevard at an outdoor restaurant watchin sold out afros sport by. we went to an african party with ahmed muhammad, an african friend of francisco's. i danced to african music with african men all of whom were much shorter than i—while francisco stood in a corner most of the evenin eyein this beautiful dark brown black girl wearin a bright orange dress designed with the back out.

we had dinna at cafe figaro's on melrose with raoul and susan, the married french couple from france, who were makin a film in Hollywood. they had seen francisco's film in sausalito at the house-shack and told us to look them up when we came to l.a.; they were very interested in the progress of francisco's film, and invited us to stay with them at their house, in paris, if we eva came. our lost weekend, was a good weekend.

MONDAY
screen room time at beverly hills hotel—four o'clock. banks were opened so me and francisco got fifty dollars out the bank. money at last.

we drove to the l.a. international airport to pick up his illustrious supa stuck up snob just recently divorced sista who flew in for a few days to have a fling. she kept askin me seriously to introduce her to some of my hollywood star friends.

we drove to the beverly hills hotel, or shall i say i drove—my drivin was bad that day. no wonder we didn't get killed cause i asked for it several times weavin in and out of the traffic.

arriving at the beverly hills hotel, the man at the gate asked us if we had so gloriously arrived to deliver somethin.

we parked our car, found our way to the screenin room walkin down elegant hallways of glass and little plastic shops, green carpets, stuffed women, and manicured men—chris arrived. i caught a glimpse of her hoppin down the stairway with her dog lisa, and dave pressman. yeah, they looked important alright, they looked great togetha. dave disappeared somewhere, did i say hello? i don't know i was fucked up. i could barely talk my mouth was so dry. chris introduced me to someone—was it dave's production manager? it was all i could do to manage a calm hello. dave arranged the screenin at the hotel, at chris's request, yes, dave was bald. chris said he had balded very early in his teens. he wore those thick spectacle glasses, they looked like walter mitty spectacles if one were gonna typecast the glasses, or perhaps a professor's. he wore a beautiful pair of corduroy pants (i originaly thought they were velvet, but chris corrected me later) and sandals with white socks. i thought he looked great, with character you know. so did francisco.

francisco was in the projection room i assume cause i didn't see him for a taste. a lawyer came, mitchell thompson who had been connected with several black films. several of chris's friends came. a gay man and his wife … my father came. i had invited him, but i didn't think he would actually come, but there he was surprisin the shit out of me with his peppered haired self. there were several film distributors that francisco invited. a friend of mine came. james oliver — he arrived durin the last fifteen minutes of the film. james looked good, and thin in a purple shirt. i was glad to see him, even though he was dressin a little different from the way he dressed in n.y., he use to wear this bad leather jacket, and jeans and construction boots, now he was wearin tight fittin pants. i imagine i must have acted a little like a fool, as i popped out of my seat when the film was ova, ran up to him, kissed him, and told him i had missed him and how glad i was that he came. he looked at me a little astonished to say the least. he was bright eyed and inspired behind seein what he saw of the movie. that was good.

chris and i walked out on the beverly hills hotel lawn for a while with lisa, so lisa could grunt. we talked about our men. chris talked about how dave didn't fit her image exactly and sometimes she couldn't get ready for his formal lifestyle. she wanted to quit takin diet pills, and i flashed on how i had once loved three great, wonderful men at the same time. i would have married all of them, or any one of them, and how that experience had me scattered mad wild hither and yon, and how i didn't dig on that, and chris was funky at heart, she dug a guy who played music and wore jeans, and romped in the grass, and didn't care if the house wasn't clean all the time, and she loved dave too and maybe she just didn't know what she wanted, she's been married two times already, just twenty-five. i didn't say very much. i loved francisco. i knew what i wanted. i knew i liked the way dave looked. true, he wasn't your parlor idol but he seemed to possess a gentleness about him. he seemed strong, and knew who he was, what he looked like everythin else being bullshit, besides i neva dug no man on the basis of his looks, i mean what got me in the real true run was his mind, what he did with it, and how he treated me. i really didn't know about dave, cause i really didn't know him cept for the experience i had with him that night at malibu. we returned to the screenin room feelin high though, and good. we found everyone waitin for us when we returned.

the film to my amazement was shall i say an endurance test. the sound was absolutely terrible, hell and unbearable. several scenes take place on a bus, and the sound was so excruciatingly loud, most of the dialogue was lost. the film was a strain.

i sat as the movie rolled before my eyes wonderin if i had gone crazy. was this the same film? people were moving around in their seats disgusted, several guests got up and walked out. chris's friends sat through it all, as did chris and dave. chris startin writin a critique before the first ten minutes of the film was ova, when it was ova we had a long conversation in front of the mirror in the ladies' room. chris went on and on about how the film was borin, pedantic, wordy and me with all my nonsense, and lord knows i got plenty of it—just couldn't accept totally that that film was so bad. i mean i'm always runnin off at the mouth about quality, was there quality in this film or was i nuts. i wasn't nuts. i decided there was beauty in the film, yeah the sound completely destroyed it. if francisco had only had the money, money would have made it possible for the print that was made from the workprint perfect—money would give freedom, freedom would give time. chris said she believed in him as a film director. sure, she said to me, you're right. i see his genius. can't nobody look at that film and not see it. i'd work for him tomorrow for nothin.

i didn't feel defeat. i didn't feel defeat as i watched the film. i sat through it—as one man got up and left in the middle and then returned makin a bored yawnin sound. since—he sat back down—i released it and entered into my oblivion again. or shall i say that peaceful state of facin what is, acceptin, joinin its reality, and passin on to otha moments to be felt for one scene is not composed of one element, but several. and in my determination to not feel no dramatics havin been so susceptible to them, i chose to make adjustments that eliminated them.

chris and i left the bathroom and walked down the lobby. the women eyein us curiously.

today francisco borrowed a friend's editin room—dean porter. a nigga wearin a dashiki with a red knit hat on his head. francisco re-examined his film. there are screenins tomorrow for major distributin companies, and a french distributin company.

but dave.
dave made me feel as he stood before us talkin on the phone in the screenin room, orderin drinks for the guests before the film had started that all was cool. i mean win or lose—everythin is alright.

the screenin ova. the film existed. so what else is new?

my father split home.

dave split to colorado on business.

francisco split to the hallways somewhere to talk to mitchell thompson.

francisco's sister found her way.

chris and i split to the ladies' room.

and most of us ended up meetin in the polo lounge of the beverly hills hotel.

it was great sittin there with chris and her friends eating guacamole and sippin coke. francisco wasn't with us still. i looked in my purse to find i didn't have his wallet which had the fifty dollars in it so i left the table to see if francisco had his wallet, cause i thought he had given it to me to keep in my purse. i was scared i had lost the money. i met francisco in the lobby. the glass restaurants and delicate candy stores closed. otha worlds goin on around us, our's was no big deal. he grinned. i guess i laughed, not too loud like i do usually. it wasn't the time place or feelin. somethin like hey man, where'd you get that big fine car? or hey ain't too many niggas standin around in the lobbies of the beverly hills hotel in silver high heel shoes. or was it fun, or was it fun? da-da!

francisco's film was locked inside the cinema room—he had gotten a janitor to go get the key to open it for him. there we met. two crazy niggas. one in a black velvet dress that i had sewn up the sides that very same morning, and one in a beautiful pair of velvet pants.

did they like it?

so much so that everyone at the table talked about how great the guacamole was instead.

he's crazy you know. i mean he stood there just as crazy as me laughin. i was with him even more for some uncapitalistic reason that i could not fathom. we sat in the telephone booth and talked cause he said i was talkin too loud and gettin on his nerves and besides we didn't want no one to hear what we were talkin about.

ain't no big thing. i mean what do they know. people are so crazy they callin hitler a genius that went astray, and tricia nixon is callin her father a revolutionist on the merv griffin show, and lena horne couldn't even sing when she first started out so my mother tells me, and did you know half the sex male symbols in movies are homosexuals, and james bond is bald?

the janitor arrived with the key. francisco got his film. he had the wallet. he didn't want to go to the polo lounge. he didn't feel like it.

don't feel like it?

and i'm walkin around in here with no underwear on, in a five dollar dress i got at a thrift shop and everybody's stoppin me in the hallway askin me how much did my dress cost? and tellin me how great i look. half everybody in the world is drunk at this very second, or high on somethin.

did i say all that? no ... not really, but i must have said somethin cause we walked up the stairway to the polo lounge.

he's crazy you know. he does crazy things when we make love sometimes. i mean most people get serious when they start gettin all juiced up, but francisco takes it out to a bizarre place. he pulls out his dick and says ... i'm gonna dick whip you. he starts hittin my thigh with his dick. he'll talk to my nipples. he'll talk about how one nipple gets harder before the otha, and how the otha better act right. but he loves the otha slow nipple anyway even if it doesn't, but it always does, for him.

we joined the group and ordered coke and ate guacamole and chips with chris and her friends—and listened to chris talk cause she sure was talkin fast. i was silent. not because of lack of words. i couldn't get a word in no how. if there was somethin funny said and if i heard it, i laughed. in general i ate my guacamole and was contented. by everythin and nothin. cause it was like i just woke up for the second time that day, everythin prior to belonged to its own hall of fame and deserved no more credits due.

SO CUT—

we decided to stay in the polo lounge francisco, his sister, and i after chris and her friends left to see the twilight on the beach and eat dinna.

chris invited us to come along, but we had a previous dinna date—and so we might come ova after that.

well if we did, we could bed the night.

i wanted some more guacamole and asked the waiter to bring me some. he said i already had two bowls. yes but they are empty bowls, and i would like some more please … need i compliment the joint and say the guacamole is great. well he pranced off somewhere's to be unseen. time passed. and i wondered where our order of guacamole was. so i got up and asked the man at the door, the host i assume, all dressed in a polite smile, winning black suit with crisp white shirt and bowtie—for some more.

oh certainly, in a moment. was his refrain.

well, i sat down thinkin the victory won wonderin why did i have to fight for some more guacamole in the first damn place? ten more minutes passed. as did the waiter. and i called out loud.

WAITA!

i received the attention of the waiter and everyone else in the restaurant. he approached our table in his condescendin walk.

where is my guacamole, i asked kindly.

he told me to eat the cream cheese which was still left ova, on the table. i didn't want cream cheese. i wanted guacamole as did i tell him. and off he went—

ten more minutes passed. i got up and arrogantly asked the polite penguin man in black suit again as to why my guacamole hadn't arrived.

oh it hasn't?

i sat down. the waiter passed. i called him in a deep nigga tone.

WAITA!

it sounded like hey DOG! or come ova here slave and tap dance before i put this knife in your subordinate neck.

francisco's sister asked him in a nice ladylike tone.

will you please bring the guacamole.

i said nothin.

i recognized some famous faces scattered around as i moved my eyeballs here and there rememberin that chris told us we were sittin in the second most important booth in the polo lounge. oh yeah? out of the blue francisco squinched his face laughin, this all started with my momma's supa-eight, he said. what? i asked wonderin if he had gone nuts.

the first film i ever made you know—i stole this supa-eight from my mother, and me and my friend just went out one day and started shootin everythin in sight, that we dug you know? i didn't know nothin about makin a film. but i've always believed that if you want to do somethin, you don't ask a person if you can do it—you just start doin and learn that way.

francisco's sister her name i shall not mention remained cold, hardly sayin anythin unless it was slyly negative.

i hugged francisco and asked him how he was feelin. he tickled me. he didn't have no socks on his feet. and he was sittin with his feet comin together at the toes cause see francisco is pigeon-toed.

five minutes later the waiter arrived with a dish of guacamole that looked like he had eaten out of it, along with everybody else back there in the kitchen who probably spit in it too. 1970's goin on foreva — nigga's ova here in l.a. havin to waste their energy ova some white folks' foolishness.

we left the polo lounge after completin my glass of dubonnet, francisco's coors beer, and his sister's coke. francisco drove us ova to our friend's house where we ate meatloaf, salad, and soup on a pretty glass table covered with a twin size bed sheet for a tablecloth. maybe femie is right, i thought. maybe white folks just can't help themselves. maybe that's their nature. well i wasn't goin to waste no more time on that subject, so i ate and listened to the story of ulara, our male black friend about thirty, who told us about his car accident, earlier in the day and how he was all drugged up. i played the piano, and francisco's sister took it upon herself to make fun of my dress, and insult me on several occasions as to why i wore my hair as i did. i chose to ignore her, francisco and i carried on with ulara, who is actor, writer, casting agent. he entertained us tellin us hollywood stories, who tried to commit suicide lately, who was doin what to whom. we stayed over ulara's laughin drinkin wine, till two or three in the mornin. then we drove back to malibu. on the drive back francisco refused to let me wear his jacket, even though he wasn't goin to wear the jacket. for a moment i allowed myself to think there was a conspiracy goin on, till francisco had the nerve to ask me how to get to malibu cause see he don't know how to get around l.a. too well. i told him after i sat up there in the front seat feelin really bad for a taste. but i just rolled down the window and let the wind rush through me, until francisco's sister mentioned how cold she was—then i rolled the window up.

when we arrived at chris's house, she was still up. a friend was ova, her x-husband monroe. monroe is a millionaire, at least that's what i hear—but he sure don't look like it—i mean he looks worse than i looked in n.y. when i didn't have no home. his shoes are all fallin apart sometimes—he moves and talks strange, nervous, and stutterin into long slurs for words. he's tall, with big shoulders, huge brown eyes, and a good face. i like him. francisco's sister was extremely polite towards chris. i think francisco's sister is impressed by white folks period. she said she was scared of black folks. she ought to be, the way she acts. but anyway, francisco came and told me to come to bed. i told him i wasn't sleepin with him. i told him he didn't know how to treat me. he took me out on the balcony's bitchy black night the ocean sloppin against the sand hard, the wet wind crinklin my hair—niggas think they can make the moon melt.

francisco apologized for his behavior. i asked him what was wrong with him, i was his friend. if the film business fucked with him, he shouldn't take it out on me, especially in front of his sister. was it that he didn't want his sister to know he loved me? francisco's so busy bein cool. we bid chris, monroe, and francisco's sister goodnight and slept on the sofa in the den.

opinion: equivalent to imagination. truth knows no time (it don't pay to be honest) is free of time, just is. opinions based on truth opinions based on lies. more opinions are believed than truths. more opinions based on lies control the earth. trouble is everybody thinks his opinion is the truth. the world is controlled by opinions of those who possess the powa ova the imagination of the times, people, culture, mind. communicatin opinions based on lies. we spend most of our time fightin for the better bull versus the not so good bull. bull is bull. you cannot vote for the lessa of two evils. evil is evil. the work of all good men is to make a good truth a reality. the dream of all good men. those men are usually destroyed by those who wish to maintain the opinions of the time. imagination is as limitless as many minds that are free to explore their own visions, or destinies. you only live once. why miss out on being you? in the endin sequence of francisco's film there is this old wino who stumbles into the eye of the camera. he is carryin an old bunch of newspapers wearin old scoungy worn clothes—thin with lines in his neck—almost emaciated but alive—so alive in some kind of an ironic painful way. he says didn't nobody get here from imagination. it takes two to tangle.

francisco and i stood on a street corner—broadway in s.f., down in north beach listenin to the blue drifter. francisco named him the blue drifter, his real name is pete. some folks call him walkin pete. he's an old pretty faced, fine features shinin smilin singin his songs deep black man—

ain't no river that rocks like me (his fingers run up and down the strings of the guitar as he sits on a little cardboard box, a bottle of liquor beside him, tappin his feet) ain't no wind, ocean, or land that do the jitter back and forth like my legs can. when that music gets to goin deep down in my harp

and my heart hums pitta patta
don't nothin matta no more
and i am goin free—free back to home.
(then he'd laugh and shake his head in glory, while his shy
introverted cousin, a boy about fifteen or so who goes everywhere the blue drifter goes, lifted up his head to look up at
the sky for a hot minute, feelin good. he'd be too shy to look
at the people who crowded around, throwin pennies, nickels,
and dimes. the boy had big eyes, a real big nose, huge thick
lips—black stone black dressed in old clothes, a new shiny
pair of tennis shoes.)
back to black skin shinin in sweat
curly nappy hair standin on its ends
back to sayin lordy, lordy and feelin somethin grand inside rise
and go jerky from right to left.
the heat of my soul sayin, don't you know
ain't no riva that rocks like me.

francisco wanted to put him in the movie, and asked the blue
drifter for his address, where francisco could reach him. the
blue drifter gave him an address. he wrote it down on a piece
of paper while he told us. ain't nothin worryin me. i ain't wor-
ried bout nothin.

you see those people ova there? (and he pointed to a big rich
hotel across the street). some folks that live ova there, they
offa me a record, t.v. show, big fine car for the big time man ...
but i ain't goin nowheres (the blue drifter chuckled to himself,
slappin his knee), nowhere's like that man. (his hands fell on
his guitar, while his cousin patted his feet and gay talkin tom
walked by—another old wino in baggy pants, bowtie, clean

white socks, and a neatly pressed white shirt—his shoes neatly tied, hat in hand, skipped by in his spry spirit doin a beautiful slidin easy soft shoe in time to the blue drifter's melody. the blue drifter nodded in jubilee at gay talkin tom as he glided on away.)

ain't no woman right. ain't no woman right.

you treat her right and she give you a fight.
hey honey—take your big arm off me.
hey honey—take your big arm off me.
i'm tired of you grabbin on me, like i'm the trunk of some tree.

the people laughed, and threw him nickels and dimes on the sidewalk.

i had a good mornin breakfast ova chris's house. chris and i talked about dave some more. how monroe fulfilled her to a certain point and dave did. how she couldn't choose between the two men, but kept flying back and forth. without pills she had no enthusiasm for life. how she is too big a jew to commit suicide we both laughed. i can go in an office and sell myself. i mean i could make everybody like me, cause my need was that great. after a couple of days i shut off from a guy. shuttin off is normal. i think. i get tired of myself. i said, so why should i expect not to get tired of anotha person. why should i expect more from somebody else, than i can give myself.
i'm afraid of being borin.
but chris was runnin around early in the morning in a bathin suit and thongs. happy. she likes to have houseguests. francisco's sister slept in the little bedroom with the single bed.

in the mornin his sister came in the den and told us to get up, while she stared at me sittin on top of her brother, doin you know what.

we fixed some eggs and bacon and toast and ate on paper plates. i didn't feel like seein no real live dishes. then the three of us split and hung out in baldwin hills with francisco's family. there was good food, a swimmin pool, his uncle harold was there the lawyer, who also serves as francisco's lawyer for his film). uncle harold asked me how the screenin had gone.

francisco and i went swimmin. yeah, i looked good in that borrowed bathin suit. i was voluptuously skinny that day somehow. what a beautiful man francisco is. yeah, i was fine. francisco was proud of me. how did he feel. he is strong. then we went to another house. a relative of uncle harold's wife. they were black, but every one of them looked white to me. my stomach was full of ribs, chicken, potato salad, plenty of wine, and soda. i wanted to go home and see my dad. i missed home. as i went from house to house i missed my own. i missed s.f. too. cole street. i wanted to go to s.f. and just be with francisco. within my own home, was it my home? he said i was his lady didn't he? someone looked me straight in the eyes, francisco's uncle harold and called me jive.

that's nothin to get upset about. but i did. it just hit me at the right time while francisco wiggled the fat on my arm, askin me if i wanted some cold duck. i screamed no. i want to go home.

francisco and i left to take me home.

i never almost cried. i haven't cried in a long time. i haven't cried ova nothing. no man. nothin. i did almost almost. it was almost me. the me when i didn't know anything, but thought i knew everythin. me, when i was a kid you know. there was this part of me that was unprotected, still not hardened and tough. a part of me that hadn't been hurt so much that it was unbearable to feel pain. but i didn't cry. i just looked out the window and saw that girl with two long braids walkin in the rain talkin to her secret invisible lova. the rain would shield her and she felt she could talk to her invisible love and no one would hear her cause the rain's sound would surround her, and cover her voice while the cars splashed down the street—and the girl who use to sit in a.p. english and write poetry instead of takin notes on how to write a correct essay. that girl who would cry at somethin silly in a movie—the one who use to make mud pies in long island, n.y. with her ballet shoes on.

francisco drove along. the blue sky tinted in purpleness sun waving its see you tomorrow goodbye. francisco in his tennis shoes, makin funny faces at me.

you keep it up, and i'm gonna dick whip you. then i laughed and laughed and laughed.

when francisco got me home, he went straight to the bathroom. i sat behind the bar on a stool with my legs restin on the bar table—my shoes off, my feet exposed. my father had some of his friends ova. i noticed when yvonne and rochelle came half stumblin, half twirlin in through the back door drunk-happy and in their forties lookin rather good in their modern-hip clothes, up to date hairstyles, and sandals—toe-nails that came to sharp points painted red. rochelle was tall and reminded me of my mother. she was dark like my mother, much taller, broader shoulders—her movements much more country whereas my mother's movements are very refined when she talks, or walks. rochelle didn't handle herself with the same aristocratic air that my mother strides through this world with. but her face was like mom's, the eyes and nose, and lips fell in the same places, kind of doin the same thing. rochelle was nice and friendly, talkin bout how this was a lovely house, all it needed was some love.

yvonne went on about how i hadn't changed a bit since i was a kid, and how she knew this young black man, rich and all not your regular run of the mill man of these times, she emphasized—who would marry me on the spot. and how i was breakin my father's heart by not goin to college, and how she introduced my father to rochelle, and how she hoped i didn't mind, but my father is so lonely. rochelle giggled and told yvonne to mind her own business and then rochelle moved her hands in a dancer's gesture that was very much like my mother—or was i just thinkin about that woman. mom was gone.

so was my sister. anne left with her. anne is goin around with some young man my mother doesn't approve of, i hear. oh everybody is the same in the end, i once said. yes everybody is the same in the end, my mother agreed, but in the meantime.

my motha's a nut. she likes little antique things of quality as she puts it. she got this house here touched with all kinds of shit. i mean it took her a whole year to furnish the livin room. she use to get up every saturday mornin—i'd get up with her sometime—we'd go on the bus cause my father got tired of drivin my mother around for what seemed to be a light year for mom to find the perfect sofa, chairs, etc. mom didn't like to drive. she walked in and out of stores in beverly hills, disenchanted with the lack of quality. why should she spend her money on somethin that wasn't right?

and so she'd tell the salesman, or saleslady somethin as to thank you very much, but the material just isn't up to par. usually the sales person looked at my mother condescendingly at first. i mean it didn't matter how well she looked—or the fact that she didn't work in no furniture store on saturday to make no livin (my mom did look well, distinguished with taste you know. never over done, or nothing, just simple) it was just the idea that she was black, and how could she possibly afford to buy furniture in these stores. i mean she wasn't no movie star, singer, or famous black football player.

francisco came out of the bathroom and saw my feet, went and got two pieces of french bread and put my feet between them like a sandwich, then took a big bite into my toes. yvonne and rochelle witnessed this act with eyes bulging, some more friends of mine came ova—art and some dude friend of his sportin an al capone hat, and a cool don't need you attitude— too big and bad to talk, just stare you down.

francisco started talkin bout how a blippie is a black hippie. a blofographer is a black photographer. i caught on sayin, a blicture, was a black picture, and whispered blussy was black pussy. then francisco asked,
what's a blimp?
art said a black pimp.

francisco shook his head, starin us all in the eye and answered with cool nonchalance.
a black imp.

we all looked at francisco stone-faced while he cracked up and then everyone else cracked up too, two seconds later ... after it sunk in. i mean who ever heard of a black imp? but there we all were laughin. i threw a paper napkin at francisco while he flirted with rochelle and yvonne. he like to make the lovely ladies smile, he like to make em feel good. this house needs love, yvonne said lookin at me. sure it's a great big house, but it's fallin apart. the curtains are raggedy, the plaster is chippin off from the ceilin.

My father stumbled in through the back porch door with Mark and a lady friend of Rochelle's visiting her from Chicago. The lady had red hair, and they called her Carrot. She was wearing a green pants suit, and must have been in her thirties, freckles all over her light brown face—little red freckles. She almost tripped as she came in the house announcin in her extremely deep voice,

It's a woman's perogative to change her mind.

Art took a sip of strawberry hill wine. He was goin away to the armed forces on friday. The f.b.i. had been on his case for two years cause that's how long he dodged the draft.

Yvonne was tellin her husband Mark how much she loved him.
I buy you your clothes.
They're out of style, Mark snapped.

She loves you, Carrot interrupted loud and unruly sounding almost like a man … and she wants you to be beautiful. You should accept it.

I don't accept it. I contest it. I got to make up my own mind.

Men don't have any minds, Rochelle said lightly wandering from room to room waving a piece of chicken in her hand.

When you a woman, and you love a man you want him to be Beautiful, Carrot chimed ova and ova.

My father laughed.

Respect. You want respect not love.

You need money to get love.

Love? Rochelle laughed hysterically … Oh don't be ridiculous, what's that?

Maybe you don't need money to get love, but you need money to keep love.

You ain't got no money!

Well, I know what gets respect, Rochelle stated pointing her chicken bone in the air with authority.

Money … everybody respects money, honey!

I can take care of all my women, Mark shouted.

What women? What all women are you talkin about man?

This house has such lovely things, Rochelle let out still wandering around in the livin room nonchalantly, occasionally bumping into my drunk father, eating the chicken bone.

Look at this little lamp over here Carrot.

I have sistas! Mark defended himself mightily, almost losing his balance. They're my blood. We bleed togetha!

Do they help pay your bills? Yvonne screamed, and then gasped for breath cause she reached to grab at Mark's neck violently, but she was too drunk, too high.

Those who bleed togetha should live togetha.

Sistas can't do what a wife can do, Carrot said with her hand on her big hip, shakin her lopsided booty.
That all depends upon what kind of sista you talkin about.
Oh, shut up man.

Rochelle's daughter arrived with a low cut tight fitting sweater on, no bra, and wanting to go swimming. Mark's eyes bulged with excitement and desire when he looked at that young thing. Yvonne got upset and told Rochelle's daughter that she shouldn't go around without a bra, that she was askin for trouble.

You mean, I'm givin you trouble ... Oh Yvonne, relax, the dark-skinned, lavishly eye made up, red fingernail polished cigarette smoking girl-woman smiled. i don't want your husband.

Mark and my father had been gone by this time. Francisco and I sat on the couch togetha, his arms around me. I listened as I rested my head on his shoulder.

Rochelle and her daughter split to the backyard, where I guess her daughter went swimming. I think the men followed after to oversee the sights (meaning Mark and my dad).

See this all started when we were in the backyard talking about our problem.

Carrot sat down and shook her head, murmurin oh lord ... oh lord.
What's that? Art asked gulping down some more strawberry hill wine.

Our problem? Yvonne asked introspectively.

He won't do anything i ask. Nothing.

Francisco pinched me. I pinched him back while Art laughed, and the gangster remained cool. Yvonne stared me straight in my eyeballs.

Row ... row ... row ... your boat.

gently down the stream.

Merrily, merrily, merrily, merrily.

life is but a dream.

No! Yvonne stood up screaming. No, No, No you see i married him because he did everything I asked him to do. He was so wonderful. And I said to myself, I can't lose now. I got a winner, cause you see I'd been married before. Now—he won't do anything I ask.

Why? I asked.

Well you see (she pointed her fingers to me, talking explicitly), it's a terrible thing when outsiders interfere with a couple's marital life.

(Art rolled his eyes. The room was silent. We all listened to her intently—she had the floor.)

See, his brother told him he was henpecked cause he did everything I asked him to do.

But didn't you do what he wanted you to do? I asked.

Yes ... yes ... of course. Of course. and I told him. I told him—

I do what you want me to do—we share. We give. You ask me to do something and I do it. But he wouldn't listen. His brother planted that seed in his mind and that was that. And so now (she winked her eye at me and smiled triumphantly making a free gesture with her arm in the air), I don't do anything he asks me to do. I fixed him. It's been like that for ten years now. If he says, where's the plyers? I just say, oh I don't know. They're around here somewhere. Why don't you look for them, and that's "Our Problem." (And then Yvonne left the living room in a skip calling lovingly after her husband.)

Part V

Fat Funky Martha Says, She's Gonna Kill Herself. She Ain't Got Nothin to Live For. Tell Her She Got Plenty to Live For. Tell Her to Live to Lose Three Hundred Pounds, and to Take a Bath Every Now and Then.

me, francisco, summa day.
we went swimmin in my pappy's pool. i was naked. felt good.
came in the house. sat on a stool by the bar. francisco was hard.
i asked him who was it for?

we went upstairs and laid on my bed. the telephone rang. ova
and ova. it was exavier calling, from s.f. to say he had arranged
for some meetin between francisco and some bank folks.

fuck a bank, fuck a movie. fuck me.

we got up instead and went to jim morrison's editin room,
where francisco sat and re-examined his film. jim was talkin
bout how *staggerlee*, one of francisco's earlier films is a classic.
jim also told me i had the feelin of a thirty-year-old woman. i
didn't know how to take that statement.

then we went to his apartment. ova in the highland-hollywood area, near the hollywood freeway, and closer to the smog. jim's apartment reminded me very much of n.y. it was small, would-do, that was about all, without roaches. and a window looked out ova the gas fumed l.a. freeways.

jim showed us a film of zanzibar on a wall, in his small closet — all the clothes pushed to the one side. i could see why francisco wanted to shoot his western in africa. francisco lived in botswana — a country where they give you a chicken every time you leave. at least they gave francisco a chicken every time he would come and go. he built a two-story hut there out of bricks and straw. as i looked at the film, i saw these incredible land-animals man ... wild animals, some crazy nigga cowboys with guns, on horseback — africans naked or in their respective style of dressing, one half-indian half nigga with a top hat on, and james brown in concert at a neighboring african village turning the women on.

chris. i met her at paramount studio two years ago, shortly before i left impulsively for n.y. i was goin to the beverly hills health club taking sauna baths, and exercising on machines, occasionally listening to the neurotic old rich and young rich. the old rich committed to their neocolonialism. the young rich feeling guilty because they knew they were the neocolonialism, confused as to what to do with their lives. life having no goal, cause the american dream (goal) was already conquered for them. listening to white women informing me as how they were darker than me. (yeah, but i don't have to work at it.)

i went to paramount studio that one day cause i had just finished a guest-starrin role on a t.v. show filmed at their studio a week before — so the guard knew me at the gate, and would let me in without any trouble. and i felt like hangin out havin nothin to do with myself, or so i thought at the time — maybe besides the fact that there was this guy workin there that i dug. he was white, son of a famous actor, and he was pretty much on his way to bein famous hisself. i mean his doors were already open, and he wasn't even that good. but he could play the piano. man, could he play the piano. everythin from jazz to classical, and the things he would improvise. in those days black men i knew, and unfortunately they were mostly actors (so my circle was limited) didn't look at black women lessin they had some money and they looked to grey women for that anyway. for a long time, i could have gone around wonderin what was wrong with me. when i think back if i had followed all the professional advice given me, lord knows what i would look like now. once i was told i must shave my eyebrows if i wanted to be an actress, cause they were too thick.

anyway, chris was an old friend of that guy, and she came to visit him on the set too. chris had just arrived from n.y. she was dressed in a blue t-shirt, clean raggedy jeans, rich leather boots, carrying a leather bag with otha clothes in it. while our friend worked, we talked in his dressing room, ate doughnuts and drank coffee.

when we decided to leave, i gave her a lift home, in jane my car — a beautiful green 1967 volvo. jane is dead now, but then she was cool. chris was all tripped out behind her apartment

on hollywood blvd, cause it was huge with a stairway lead-
ing up to a large bedroom with windows looking out on the
bushes, trees and houses across the street. a lovely living room,
good sized kitchen, little dining room area, ornate bathroom,
all for one hundred and fifty dollars. she said in n.y., such a
place would cost a fortune. maybe she was twenty-two or
three then. she was living with a thin nineteen-year-old boy-
man named jimmy—pimpled face and kind who she loved at
the time. i had just broken up with a man i had lived with for
a year. a golden-tanned irish-mexican man who introduced
me to bob dylan, full moons, candlelight dinnas as an ordinary ritual and not a special one, disdain for banks, insurance
companies, and the concept that any salary over ten thousand
dollars a year was blood money, along with camping out at
kern river and swimmin in the strong riva tides, catchin fish
and eatin it out there in nature. i don't know, chris and i just
hit it off.
i mean, you can talk about grey folks all you want, and i'll talk
with you but chris and i just transcend that, and yet meet it.
francisco thinks she's high strung, and talks a lot which is true
now and then. but it wasn't so true then. she had just come to
hollywood then, she's been here three years now. it's strange
and strange some more. she is just someone i am not afraid to
love, someone who does not remind me of how.

i only saw chris three or four times before i up and flew to n.y.
she let me stay in her n.y. apartment near 77th and madison
avenue, with a model friend subleasing the place named sessa.
sessa was from sweden, and appeared on the covers of the top
magazines like vogue and bazaar. i had neva seen anyone that
thin in my life. i had never met anyone that moved and talked

in such foreign ethereal slow motion. i had neva met anyone knowingly who shot heroin before.

n.y.—it was the first time in my life that i had seen black men in theatre, in art—who loved black women. and i mean black women who were proud of the structure of their faces, bodies and in no way desirous of the white concept of beauty. i don't know, this probably sounds naive and stupid, but i went to n.y. and discovered a whole alternative culture of black women completely different from the career-driven false eyelashed, birth control pilled, shaved under the arms, on the legs—wigs, and more wigs suck anybody's dick to make it black women, that i was generally exposed to in l.a., tinsel town u.s.a. not to say that's the only place they have women like that, it's just that i had neva had seen it nowheres else on such a large, dedicated scale. those women were gentle, strong, spoke softly, wore rings in their noses, *geles* that extended high upon their heads wrapped triumphantly, unashamed of their big black hips and booty, but movin in flowin black elegance, and grace. i mean there are kinds of women in the world, that for the first time i saw just because maybe my eyes were wide open excitingly ta-kin everythin in, bein in n.y., the first day swept me up and took me away. imagine neva even seeing a picture of a state you were born in, living in l.a. where everything is spread apart, and basi-cally modern, and suddenly waking up one morning in a mad-cap cocktail city, of new world buildings, old raggedy streets where you can see immigrants in spirit walkin down the street beside you. i went in and out of every store on fifth avenue, roamed all ova harlem first only seeing its beauty, its magic, slowly seeing its pain. walkin along streets filled with nothin but black folks mostly, and rock n roll blastin from record shops, keepin you in musical rhyme, and the lower east side, the artists, the musicians, the madness. lately, i've seen white models in vogue and bazaar posin with rings in their noses, afro bush hair-styles, and *geles* wrapped around their heads.

francisco visited muhammad one afternoon. muhammad lives in silverlake. anyway, muhammad says it is time for women to work, and men to rest.

we're ova muhammad's now. this guy named frank is ova here too. a black too, big bushy afro, and beads around his neck talkin bout how he use to be into white women. he tripped that trip once. now he totally rejects white women.

yeah, well—always a radical convert.

muhammad says james brown is a true black american artist. the television is on—the sound off. jazz is playin out of a radio box, we're watchin this movie bout how this clown loved this woman, and comes home and finds her with another man and almost kills her and the dude. but he doesn't. he is succumbed by the arms of several men who arrive on the scene from no-where, and alas is taken away. he sure did love that woman, frank says.

yeah, but chumps always get wasted, francisco says. muham-mad offered us some coffee. john lee hooker is playin at pre-mium jazz, tonight. you want to go? i want to go dancing. i want to go dancin at the black orpheus, dancin frees my spirits, and my bones, and my head—everything. i saw these young bloods dancin on soul train this mornin. they were gettin down. i mean them mommas were doin it. chris was watchin the spooks on t.v. she got up and left, said they'd give her a complex. it is six o'clock. francisco has been talkin to producers about *green front t.v. fixed up*. one is a nigga and says money ain't no problem, white folks ain't ready that he don't need them. the otha is a jew, who wants to do the movie, but is hesitant that francisco is too young, inexperienced, and not the son of no famous black man. don't no jew want to entrust no half million dollars, to no twenty-seven-year-old black dude. besides he wants to make sure francisco likes him as a friend and doesn't just want his money. and i worked in a friend's movie last week, and made two hundred dollars for two days work. the magic of life is that it does change. that you can't say because a man is a drunk, career ended, in jail, that his future is dead. you can't say that marilyn monroe did herself a blessin by killin herself, because her career was ova, had she lived she'd be a de-escalated once-star, how many times married, drinkin drinkin. who is to say somethin wouldn't have come into her life, that she could of moved to connecticut and wrote books? neva listen to the defeatest attitude, havin more faith in death than in life is neva a man—a song to listen to. white folks like to be around niggas cause we know how to have a good time. they got to think about it.

it is six o'clock. i slept on my daddy's couch last night in my clothes with a blanket ova me, after turnin off the t.v., i turned off the night.

francisco slept ova his uncle harold's house, who lives in hemosa beach. he called at ten-thirty this mornin to say hi, and to ask me if i wanted to go to the screenin with him.

yes i did. he would be ova in an hour.

larry called he wanted to go swimmin. sure.

donald chambers called tellin me how he was goin to do this t.v. show, would i be in it? sure.

francisco came ova. i had been dreamin. i dreamed about a man who came and took me away. i woke up.

francisco.

i was glad i was in my house and it was just a dream.

francisco.

after openin the door, i ran upstairs and put on my white pretty robe. though my hair looks like topsy, cause i haven't combed it since july 4th, he hasn't said anything about my hair. francisco came in the house. he looked good. real good. like he had gotten some good rest. he looked thinna. i fixed him some breakfast. i put too much oil in the fryin pan for the eggs, so i wiped the eggs off with a napkin, when they were done—so they wouldn't be so oily. we ate.

i got dressed, then we went off to c.f.i. to screen his movie for two distributors who neva showed up.

francisco had the screenin room for an hour. we waited forty minutes. no one came. do you eva stop yourself when somethin is right, and keep on going when you feel somethin is wrong? sure i'd like to take that one hundred and fifty dollars i have in the bank and go to n.y. just for a day. shit yeah—but francisco is right. francisco got the two thousand dollars for editor's option. francisco worked awful hard to get the money to do his film. i mean he must have wanted to do it awful bad to go through all he went to do it. but he's incredible. francisco wants to go to s.f. we're goin this weekend. he has to give editor the money for the option then he has all these people lined up to talk to. everythin else may fall by the wayside, but francisco goes on.

(i remember what i want to remember, i forget what i want to forget. that's the only way i can stay afloat. and the rest you don't care about. i laughed ... right, he said smiling, right.) mirth may it fill you mighty mustached man of impressed height and beauty. we went to pizza boza, this pizza place over in silverlake, a section near the downtown where mexicans, and grey folks, black folks, and all kinds of folks live togetha cool. we ate pizza and drank some beer, and i cracked up listening to francisco's stories about when he stopped workin at this news t.v. show, where he was a star reporter, and tried to get into film school, and couldn't. why? i asked. i dont' know, they didn't like my films i guess. they didn't like this treatment i wrote. i don't know. so what did you do? i decided to make ain't nobody slick, and lied so i could get into the jail to interview angela. and he cracked up laughin. i mean i fail, but i go on tacklin bigger things. and about the days at stanford, all his friends were jammin girls, and girls were droppin frogs down toilets, and he became head cheerleader, he was a romanticist, never had the urge for sex. but when he came back from africa he changed, and was jammin from right to left to the amazement of all his friends, like ken milliard, who wore an afro that came to a point, and bell-bottoms before folks even wore afros, before folks even wore bell-bottoms.

then we stopped talkin, because we both became depressed. so we just ate and looked out the window. some kids came in the restaurant and asked me for my autograph thinkin i was somebody else. i told them i wasn't who they thought i was.

francisco drove me to a safeway supermarket where i bought mascara for my eyelashes figurin i might as well try to make myself look halfway decent considerin i'd been walkin around with my hair uncombed wearin the same outfit for three days straight. i put the mascara on in the store, and felt cool. then bought us a paper cause we was on our way to the movies to see this black film. we found the theatre house in westwood, near the u.c.l.a. campus, entered. francisco got his traditional popcorn. i got some orange soda. we sat and waited. the film began. we sat through it—when we left we felt great.

francisco had a film, that's all, i mean i *shit* through, i sat through that piece of film of a movie and wondered the whole time now how in the world can they reject francisco's film. a movie that was made full of truth. a movie that a person would come and watch and be inspired from, a movie a person could be entertained by and still relate the humanness in the film, to their own lives. okay, superman godzilla king kong runnin through the jungle, rippin women off animal—okay less than human shit. learn from bad example, possible, learn from good example possible. as i write this, i get more and more pissed. i mean where, how did all these people get into powa who keep pushin all this garbage down our throats, who do we let them think we are? and how can we allow them to make us such shit, by our payin our hard-earned nickels and dimes, or sittin on our behinds watchin it. we accept it. not only do we accept it. we pay money for garbage. we pay money to look, laugh at, enjoy, and talk about did you see that garbage last week on channel so and so wasn't it great? art can turn back the work of a people. entertainment has influence on the political moods of a people. movies can destroy all the work gone down, and make it cool to have no goals, to feel it's noble to be poor, black, and strong, and excitin to be immoral, unprincipled, rich, and black. you can't separate it from influencin the images (and lack of content, or content) of a searchin mind. francisco's a nigga walkin around, runnin around in this crazy, fucked-up beautiful world tryin to do somethin about it, workin hard to do somethin about it. workin hard to put his film out there and i believe in him and will do everything in my powa to help him. his first major film effort or are we so weak that we have forgotten about creativity, inspirin the character of man—enlightenin man toward the workins of a positive alive life that is good value, quality, carin, truth. borin. they got us thinkin to express beauty in life is borin. unsensational. did they push that horror—rape, asshole bullshit down our throats so long that we think if we ain't lookin at that, and doin that life is borin? yeah, i don't want to be in those films. if i live in a world where love is not projected as a value, then wouldn't i tend to believe that it don't exist? how am i to know about love, if in what is projected through art, creativity (so-called) states that love don't exist. revealin life, revealin the slimy parts along with the good is necessary, but gloryin the dirt is anotha story. so i might as well sell whatever whole i got workin, if it's still workin cause i don't care about nothin—that's right, and nothin is worth carin about anyway. i might as well sell pussy for whatever the goin price is. a woman and a man togetha is a rare thing. all the black princesses walkin around america don't even know they're princesses, talkin loud with natural combs stuck in the back of their heads. but i won't sell it. i'll just go on and walk through these streets believin in what i believe, cause at least i know i have somethin to believe. at least i know i have somethin to believe in that means somethin to me, even if it don't mean nothin to you all there in control—who's only powa is your mediocrity threatened by us who bring, offa the gift of art for the survival of the human heart.

we should all kick ass and get this mess cleaned up. till it's free and open and clear to breathe and eat and enjoy the earth again.

we drove to a restaurant, feelin good. we sat in the restaurant drinkin tea and coffee. francisco had some french fries. i neva met nobody that don't like ketchup on french fries—nothin but a pound of salt. that's how he likes it.

francisco guessed he was a bad loser, someone told me once a good loser never wins. the person who said that was fucked up though so i said you ought to be a bad loser, cause you ain't suppose to lose anyhow. i was mad. but i didn't know how to say what i really meant at the time. i just had this feelin that somethin was wrong somewhere—francisco must be lazy or in a rush, or either too slow. i didn't know, but i talked too much that was for sure and everythin i said was wrong.

quincy bennet, an acquaintance of francisco's came in the

restaurant and sat up talkin about francisco's movie. he didn't know none of the changes francisco had been through. he just stumbled in from off the streets somewhere and remembered seein francisco's film somewhere and started askin how was it doin, givin francisco advice about how to do this, how to do the otha, some of what he said was good, some of it was bad. at times he put francisco down talkin bout when you enter for the big dough you ain't entering a world of boys and how he ought to get his shit togetha, and well that's true—but everybody should just do that naturally foreva. he looked at me, and said i was makin francisco cool.

francisco is cool by his own self.

it amazed me how even yesterday francisco and i sat on my father's couch—my father wasn't home, finding peace together after all this mess—francisco was a strong dude, that was as graceful in struggle as he is when everythin is honky-dorry. quincy bennet said francisco was a born winner. how everythin he wanted was all there waitin for him. all he had to do was go out and get it.

we split the restaurant and drove home.
quietly to my father's house. francisco kissed me and slept in the maid's room. i lay on the couch in the den for a while. but then i wanted to be with francisco. so i got up, walked through the kitchen, through the back porch into the bathroom, and entered the maid's room.

francisco, may i sleep with you for a while?
no he said ... no.

Part VI

You Can Stick It in Me, Through Thick and Thin

francisco packed up all his clothes, his film and shit and after dinner at figaro's, after driving me home to my father's house—after pickin me up and throwin me around in circles in the street—got in his car and drove home to cole street, he left me in l.a.

he's gone
and all i can think about is that morning i lay in the bed beside him in malibu. exavier was still with us, the three of us were gettin along havin a good time … but i lay in the bed upset, cause i don't know i'm a girl and i get upset when it's been for so long. i told francisco i was goin. i was leavin. i got up out of bed and he said if you go home you can't come back.

i love you, he said … i never lived with a woman before it's gonna take time for me to adjust … it's not easy. i guess it ain't easy—yeah, it ain't easy livin with a man either. and so i was happy takin a shower with my old man. the water runnin ova our brown bodies, he looked so good in the water—i was washin him down the front of his chest along his shoulders and arms with a cloth rich in soap.

you have to stay with me through thick and thin, he grinned.

i was willin. i neva said i was willin but i was. maybe you don't
need money to get love or keep it. maybe you need to know
when to open your mouth and when to keep it shut. but i got
a good mind to go up there and kick his big black ass for leavin
me down here in all this heat and smog by my own self. but i
won't—yes i will ... oh shit!

a week later.
chris stopped takin diet pills and george eves died from an
overdose of heroin at his own party in berkeley in his apartment at age twenty-one. james oliver flew in from n.y. again a
couple of days ago. the film he was goin to direct was canceled
(the one i was goin to be in remember?) but the same motion
picture studio is negotiating for him to direct anotha. james
took me to see richard the third at the mark taper forum. when
he brought me back home, i ran upstairs to say hi to my dad
and to ask if francisco had called me. but my dad read this
whole thing you have just read, and ordered me out of his
house, after askin me what kind of girl am i?

yesterday i woke up and found i had broken out all ova my
body with these incredible bumps and sores. i've stayed inside
mostly and only taken walks to this restaurant down the street
that has newspaper pasted on its walls for wallpaper. there i
have broiled salmon, broccoli, and tea every now and then. i
sleep well. but i usually wake up in some kind of fit. generally
i notice, the pillows, and blankets, are strewn to every end of
this hotel room.

i mean i woke up at eleven this mornin, after layin round rollin
round, tossin and turnin round with this friend of mine. me.

Afterword

though the ending of this book is left unresolved ... the broken, youthful journey/search for truth, meaning, purpose, belonging clarity, safety, and most passionately of all love ... continued ...

three years after this book was published, like the woman remembered in luke 7:38 i also came weeping to Jesus, washing his feet with my tears, drying his feet with my wooly hair, anointing his feet with oil, sinned much, forgiven much, and Loved much by Yahwe in the midst of it all ... when i look back i now see His implicit presence ... He was there all the time as the old gospel tune illuminates ... as i was seeking He was seeking after me passionately with His fresh mercies, calling me His ... gently whispering You are Mine ... i remain eternally grateful every day for His suffering shed blood for my sins, saving of my lost soul, bringing me out of darkness and giving me revelation of His Eternal Word ... He is my foreva Shepherd, my Jesus.

i have struggled with the release of this book due to the profanity, lifestyle of fornication, that i no longer endorse. as i acknowledge my youthful sins, i also look back in gratitude to my younger, free-spirited self for making a few choices that kept me alive ... to her i say thank you.

so i tenderly let go in the hope that the knowledge of my encounter with Christ and activating power of Holy Spirit transformation in my life can somehow give Glory to Yahweh and encourage others in their search for truth. Try Jesus. He is the way, truth, and life. no man comes to the Father but through Him.

five years after this book was written francisco made peace with Yeshua, repented of his sins, befriended humble righteousness and came looking for me requesting marriage. he was a faithful, compassionate husband, caring, present father to five beautiful children, changed diapers, helped around the house, and cooked the best fried fish and french fries like nobody's business. he served as pastor/evangelist (persecuted for his faith: spit on, his life threatened, fired) with me by his side, took roses to prostitutes on sunset blvd telling them God loved them, carried a cross he built himself in washington square park (and cannes film festival, reported by e! entertainment), took in and fed the homeless, preached to young gangbangers, drug addicts, rich poor black white, all humans without partiality ... wealthy with healing faith and loving kindness, never met a stranger kind of dude.

francisco was adjunct professor of film studies at chapman university. he taught history of documentary film, history of african american cinema and film production and cultural heritage (where because he was black was mistaken for a transient by campus police who refused to believe he was a professor, and demanded he leave the premises).

his films include *Staggerlee: A Conversation with Black Panther Bobby Seale* (1970), *Ain't Nobody Slick* (1972), the award-winning *Virgin Again* (2000), and *Straight Out of Compton* (2001). he worked construction jobs and taught as a substitute teacher … he loved to teach, and was so popular with his students they packed out his homegoing celebration from wall to wall. Francisco passed away May 22, 2003 unexpectedly. we were married till death do you part.

ALISON MILLS NEWMAN

MAY 2022

ALISON MILLS NEWMAN started her career as the first African American teenage actress on a television series (*Julia*). As a musician and vocalist, she has performed with Ornette Coleman, Don Cherry, Weather Report, and Taj Mahal. She is an award-winning film director and the author of the novel *Maggie 3*. Mills Newman is the President of Keep the Faith Film Ministries and a chaplain at Fulton County Jail, and has five beautiful children with the late Francisco Toscono Newman, as well as ten grandchildren.

SAIDIYA HARTMAN is the author of *Wayward Lives, Beautiful Experiments, Lose Your Mother: A Journey Along the Atlantic Slave Route,* and *Scenes of Subjection.* A MacArthur Fellow, she is University Professor at Columbia University and lives in New York.